The Blacksmith's Daughter

A

Standalone

Dystopian Romance

Guy S. Stanton, III

Words of Action

Guy's books can be found in a variety of formats, both digital and print, at the following locations: A Warrior's Pen, Amazon, Barnes&Noble, Smashwords, Apple iBookstore, and Kobo.

Professional Editing Performed By: Phyllis Neely
Her Contact Info: fanyika@gmail.com

Cover Artist: The Author
Note: I now design book covers. If interested in a book cover designed by me feel free to get in touch at the email address listed below.

Author's Website: https://www.a-warriors-pen.com
Note: My website is currently not available. It will be hopefully renovated soon.

Comments – Reviews – Ratings: **Always Appreciated!**

Contact Info: guysactionwords@gmail.com
Goodreads Page: Guy Stanton III
Facebook Page: https://www.facebook.com/guysactionwords
YouTube Channel: Words of Action – Christian Fiction at its Best!

The Blacksmith's Daughter / Guy S. Stanton, III. – First Edition.

Available Books

The Warrior Kind *Series*

Book 1: A Warrior's Redemption
Book 2: A Warrior's Journey
Book 3: A Warrior's Legacy
Book 4: A Warrior's Return
Book 5: A Warrior's Revenge

The Agents for Good *Series*

Book 1: Agent with a History
Book 2: Agent for a Cause
Book 3: Agent out of Time
Book 4: Agent in the Dark
Book 5: Agent on the Run
Book 6: Agent finds a Warrior

Water Wars *Series*

Book 1: Journey into the Deep
Book 2: The Proverbial War
Book 3: The Quest for Paradise

The Wind Drifters *Series*

Book 1: Fire Wind
Book 2: Ice Wind
Book 3: Hard Wind
Book 4: Rift Wind
Book 5: Drift Wind

Fire Prophets *Series*

Book 1: The Way
Book 2: The Truth
Book 3: The Life, Coming Soon

The Kainos Warriors *Series*

Book 1: Dissonant Times
Book 2: Out of This Time, Coming Soon
Book 3: No More Time, Coming Soon

A Man Called Mako Series

Book 1: Mako, Coming Soon
Book 2: Mako's War, Coming Soon

Non-series Books

The Kingdom
Fallen Ambitions
Pharaoh's Slave
The Blacksmith's Daughter
The Iron Maiden, Coming Soon

Non-fiction Books

A Guy's Thoughts: A Book of Personal Psalms
Flat Earth: Evidences To Consider If You Dare

Kindle Vella Stories

Raw

List updated August of 2022

General Content Advisory Warning

For my Dear Readers, who may be sensitive to certain situations and actions that can be triggering.

This story does contain all of the following:

- General Action/Apocalyptic Story Related Violence.
  Read at your own discretion.

- There are sensually romantic elements contained within this story, but nothing of an overly explicit nature. Particular sexual based sinful life-styles are also addressed from a Biblically based point of view.

Some quotes by Thomas Jefferson that are formative to understanding the premise of the world I have authored in this story. I see the need to warn others of what I see occurring at a great rate all around me. The destruction of mankind by his own hand, aided by the demons that hate them.

First Quote: *"I am not a friend to placing growing men in populous cities, because they acquire their habits & partialities which do not contribute to the happiness of their after life."*

Second Quote: *"I view great cities as pestilential to the morals, the health and the liberties of man. True, they nourish some of the elegant arts, but the useful ones can thrive elsewhere, and less perfection in the others, with more health, virtue & freedom, would be my choice."*

Third Quote: *"I think we shall be [virtuous], as long as agriculture is our principal object, which will be the case, while there remain vacant lands in any part of America. When we get piled upon one another in large cities, as in Europe, we shall become corrupt as in Europe, and go to eating one another as they do there."*

CONTENTS

Current Year: 2147

1901 AD

- The RMS Cruise Line Ship the Lucania is the first ship to receive a wireless radio set.

1927 AD

- The US Federal Radio Commission begins to regulate radio frequencies. The Commission was later renamed to be the Federal Communications Commission.

1947 AD

- On the heels of World War II the International Monetary Fund comes into being.

1963 AD

- The Hotline or 'Red Phone' is installed to provide instant communication between the USA and the Soviet Union.

1979 AD

- The National March for Gay Rights takes place in Washington. DC.

1987 AD

- Fluoxetine aka 'Prozac' is released as an approved method of dealing with depression.

1991 AD

- The World Wide Web becomes commonly available to all after being made available the prior year first to CERN (European Organization for Nuclear Research).

1992 AD

- IBM invents the first smartphone.

1997 AD

- IBM's Deep Blue supercomputer defeats world chess champion Garry Kasparov.

1999 AD

- The Melissa Computer Virus attacks Internet users' email accounts.

2005 AD

- Scientists admit to creating mice containing human neurons for the purpose of studying neurological disorders.

2015 AD

- The United Nations Climate Change Conference meets in Paris, France.

2019 AD

- The first cases of Covid-19 identified, followed by a pandemic that saw many pressured into taking an experimental vaccine aka a gene therapy mRNA shot.

2020 AD

- Worldwide fertility rates plunge, with many countries reporting below population replacement levels.

2021 AD

- China's attempt to boost fertility by allowing three children per family fails. Primary cause – refusal to marry.

2022 AD

- Study shows that the average smartphone user experiences a *'near death experience'* when they think they've lost their phone.

2023 AD

- The US Dollar falls as the world's reserve currency.

2025 AD

- Mass starvation ensues due to crop failures brought about by fertilizer scarcity and UN climate change regulations.

2029 AD

- The proxy war between NATO and the Eastern Alliance in the Balkan States and Taiwan in the East turns into a World War.

2031 AD

- Peace terms are agreed to and loans by the International Monetary Fund are issued to compliant states to rebuild infrastructure.

2047 AD

- State healthcare services are institutionalized across the world with mandatory compliance protocols put in place. Repeat offenders are deleted from the system.

2051 AD

- A World Wide Social Credit System is put into effect. Everyone is linked to an AI control center that monitors all human actions in real time in pursuit of noncompliance issues.

2059 AD

- Only the ultra-wealthy are able to afford the remaining fertility services in order to achieve a successful full term pregnancy.

2071 AD

- A huge disparity of males to females develops as no new male offspring have been born in the last 5 to 7 years.

2073 AD

- World populations riot, as it becomes clear that almost all men have been rendered sterile by electromagnetic frequency codes embedded in the AI controlled Social Credit System digital tattoo.

2075 AD

- The war known to humans as the *'Right to Live War'* comes to an end. The AI system now known as the Signal is the victor by defacto, as there are no more men left within society to mount an offensive or defensive action against it.

2076 AD

- The United Nations Climate Change Conference now comprised of all female members votes unanimously to accept the *'Guidance of Humanity Protocols'* as put forward by the AI System that has now overtaken all matters of state with the dissolution of all independent nation states upon conclusion of the war the prior year.

2077 AD

- In compliance with the Guidance of Humanity Protocols a special class of robotic enforcer known simply as a, Borg, is created to encourage the compliance of women of child bearing age with state mandated artificial insemination programs. Female only offspring are to be accepted as an approved result.

2079 AD

- Bounties are paid out to women for the successful capture and elimination of any surviving males.

2083 AD

- The voluntary insemination program is deemed a failure by the AI System and an enforcement amendment is added into the social credit score. *'Comply with reproductive initiatives or do not eat.'*

2085 AD

- The *'We have Rights!'* war concludes. All cities are turned off of all utilities and the AI controlled Borgs are turned on the remaining female population for *'Aggressive Enforcement Procedures'*.

2089 AD

- No cities remain on earth. Surviving women bind together loosely in hunter gatherer groups known as *'Colonies'*.

2091 AD

- No men have been documented or captured in over five years. Dissension breaks out within the programing code of the AI System as to how to deal with what's left of humanity. In an effort to preserve system integrity the AI System shuts the Signal down and goes offline, reliant entirely on their Enforcement Borg Division to manage the remaining women.

2137 AD

- Without AI input the Borgs initiate a failsafe system due to their numbers becoming too low for adequate enforcement over the Colonies. *'Forced artificial inseminations with female only offspring are halted.'*

2143 AD

- Another AI fail safe is initiated as Borgs continue to be decommissioned by age and the violent actions of women. *'All colonies are to be eliminated in order to stop the threat that women pose to the System, if not properly managed.'*

2147 AD

- Colonies of women only exist in select parts of Europe, Africa and the Middle East. All colonies are largely devoid of hope of anything improving, as they face complete annihilation at the insistence of the Borgs.

By year *2159 AD*, only a handful of Colonies remain within the Pyrenees regions of France and Spain. Only one Colony; however, has women yet suitable of age to give birth to children. The reason for this delayed fertility can be found in the supernatural events of *2147 AD*, which is where this story begins its narrative.

CHAPTER ONE

The Unexpected

The clanging of the hammer strikes bespoke the quiet fury felt by that of the hammer wielder. Her usual easy cadence of rhythm was off.

Typically the fall of the hammer had a rhythm all of its own, but not today. Today she was pouring forth aggression into the blade that she was crafting.

If she was not careful, she would do it harm. Her hammer poised mid strike over the heated steel that still glowed a faint red.

She did not want to bring damage to it, for if she did, it may let her or someone else down in battle. None of her weapons had ever broken, and this was not going to be the first one.

Pulling the sword away from the homemade anvil, she set her hammer down. Moving to a trough, she quenched the blade with a hiss into its cold depths.

She would work upon it again, once her temper had cooled.

Leaving her tools behind, she stepped away from the heat of the forge. She made her way to an outer post and leaned against it, and for the first time noticed the glorious quality of the new day. The sight of the sun, the sounds of the birds, and the cries of animals in the distance did much to drain away the tension she felt.

The nightmare of last night slowly let hold of its grip upon her.

The nightmare itself was nothing new. All the women had it in varying forms.

It varied little, though, in terms of its overall message, which was hopelessness.

Having the same nightmare night after night was enough to make one go mad.

In the moment of remembrance, her eyes had closed, but now they opened as she heard the sound of riders approaching. A scouting party was returning.

Only three had made it. Scouting parties were always made up of five riders.

Two more of their kind were now gone.

Her eyes widened then as she took in the diminutive form of another, not mounted on horseback. It was a child!

She stumbled as she sought to keep on her feet from what looked like clear exhaustion, even as she was tugged along by a rope about her neck.

It was no new thing to see a child abused in such a way. It was, however, odd in that of the age of the child involved. The girl couldn't be more than seven years old, eight at the most.

Most definitely less than ten years of age.

This was new. This was different.

Straightening away from the post, Amalaka stepped forward to hail the three embittered-looking riders.

"Where did you find the girl?" she asked in her characteristically deep voice.

The riders drew up with surprise. The blacksmith of the village rarely spoke, and when she did it was always something of import.

To the three on the verge of malnutrition, the blacksmith cut an imposing sight. As the blacksmith, she was the wealthiest of their community, as she made the weapons by which they all survived.

Not only that, but she made the finest weapons of any to be had by all the smithies in riding distance. She demanded respect, even as her tall muscular frame that reached well over six feet in height was its own statement, in terms of not something to be trifled with.

Respectful, the riders drew up and inclined their heads forward to her as a sign of deference. None of them owned a blade made by her, for they were the poorest of the poor, but they hoped for a weapon of hers just the same.

Her weapons came with the sufficient capableness of being able to cut through the hardened alloy shells of their robotic hunters. Such a thing was not equaled by many of her trade, and none were as fine at it as she was.

Such a weapon was not to be discounted, as it often had been the saving grace of those who were fortunate enough to wield them.

The three said in unison, "Greetings, Amalaka."

One of the three became the spokesperson. "We lost two of our number by the springs to a hobbled Borg. It could no longer move freely about, so it submerged itself under the water. We stopped to wash ourselves and it grabbed ….."

"I have no use for your sob story. You should have known better than to stop at the springs, as danger always lurks near good water. Where did you come by the child?"

Looking both taken aback and unsettled by Amalaka's aggression, the speaker said, "We fled the springs by way of the eastern forest, as we were worried that there may be more Borgs in the plains country to the west of the springs. We found her there in the forest. She does not speak our language, or at least she does not speak it well."

Amalaka glanced from them to the girl, who was weaving back and forth on her feet as she fought to remain standing. Her eyes were closed, and it was clear that she was all but done in.

The oddity of not knowing their language well was yet one more item of interest that should not be discounted when it came to this child.

Amalaka looked from the girl to her captors and flatly asked, "How much?"

The three looked among themselves with surprise. This was new to them.

Amalaka never took use of another, as in the way that had become common to many of them to do, especially for one as tall and as strong as she was.

After speculatively looking among themselves, the one said cagily, "We were about to have her for some amusement for ourselves as we drink to those forever lost to us now. After we've had our use of her, we could be moved to sell her to you for your own enjoyment as well. She is a fair one for her age, having not yet come to be like us."

Amalaka stepped forward in a long stride and repeated her question, but this time it was with a violence barely restrained. "How much?!"

It was clear to the three that the deal was to be made now.

Shaken, the one who had last spoken hesitantly said, "For three blades made by your hand, we would gladly part with her to you."

The other two glanced at her in astonishment as no girl, no matter how feminine she was in appearance, would possibly fetch such a price as that. Without hesitation though, Amalaka turned back into her shop and swiftly returned with three of her creations.

She tossed them up to the stunned riders. Then as the women beheld their payment, a blade materialized into Amalaka's hand as she severed the rope from the saddle it was tied off to. Taking a hold of it, she led the stumbling child toward her shop, even as the three riders rode off rejoicing.

The girl, whose eyes were the rarest shade of hazel, the color of them standing out starkly in a face reflecting her darker skin color, was now actively trying to resist forward progress.

Amalaka turned about, full well knowing how imposing she must seem. Her voice gentling in sound, as much as she could make it to, she said, "No harm will come to you by my hand, child."

She tugged on the rope and hesitantly the girl took a step. Once in the living quarters of her shop and away from the harsh glare of the sun outside, she swiftly tied the rope off to a post.

Tossing a cushion at the feet of the girl, she saw the girl after only a momentary hesitation collapse down upon it.

Amalaka had seen many hard things and had done them as well, but never had she abused a child. The memory of her own abuse as a child would never conscience such a thing to be done by her own hand.

Despite her long life, far longer than most, it still brought pain to her to see the disregard that had been given to this young life. It was not right.

It was just one of the many reasons that they had been damned by the God of their creation.

Gathering a pitcher of fruit water and leftovers from this morning's meal, she went to the girl and knelt down stiffly on one knee beside her.

Her own black as night skin was the darkest of any in the colony by far. The girl before her was of some similar ethnic background, albeit far lighter in complexion.

It was clear that she was a mixture of sorts, ethnically speaking, as her hair upon closer inspection was not entirely black, but had streaks of light brown; if it was cleaned, perhaps even a few blonde strands within it.

And then there were the girl's eyes.

Those mesmerizing eyes did not leave her for a second as she poured a cup full of juice and handed it out to the girl. The girl's hands grasped the cup from her and she began to glug down its contents, even as she kept one of those mesmerizing eyes focused on Amalaka warily.

"Easy child, there is more."

The cup empty, the child gasped for air. Taking the cup from her, Amalaka refilled it.

She didn't hand it back immediately, but gestured to the food on the floor.

"Eat some first."

The girl reached for a chunk of meat and brought it up with reverence to her lips, befitting the fashion of those who are famished and have despaired of ever seeing another good meal in their life. Instead of biting into it though, the girl looked from it to Amalaka.

Her cracked lips moved as she spoke for the first time. The others may not have known the girl's language, but Amalaka did. As she heard the girl's question reverberate in her mind, it caused a flood of memories to return from a very long time ago.

Amalaka was eighty-one years old. People of her ethnic background tended to age very well and Amalaka was no exception to this, other than to say she was the epitome of it.

None suspected as to exactly how old she was, and she had never told anyone. Most women did not reach past their forties. As it now was, she had lived two of their lifetimes.

She had seen much, and now at the girl's question of, '*Why?*', she remembered so much more.

Her eyes had closed. Now they opened, and taking in the girl, as emotions of the past filled into her eyes, she said in response, "Because you are special."

A moment passed by. Then with knowing wisdom she added, "You had a father."

The girl's mesmerizing eyes blinked.

"How do you know this?" she whispered.

Amalaka reached out and wiped away at a tear that had spilled down the girl's face, before admitting her own secret. "I had one, too. There is a difference between us and them out there. They have never seen a man. They have no knowledge of what it is like to have the care of a father. You know of what I speak?"

The girl nodded.

"Where is your family now?"

The girl, suddenly overwhelmed with emotion, let out with a cry, "I do not know! I was hit on the head, and when I woke up they were gone! I can't remember what happened!"

Amalaka let her head fall forward to rest against the girl's forehead, as she tried to comfort the crying child. Reaching for her neck, she carefully freed the girl of the rope tied off there, and set it down on the floor.

Tilting the girl's head up, she gently said in the girl's language, "You must stay inside. I cannot protect you, if you go out there."

The girl nodded tearfully.

Stiffly, Amalaka then moved to sit down on the floor beside her. Showing no more interest in the food, the girl instead crawled into her lap and hugged her fiercely.

It was clear that she sought out comfort over food. This priority of emotions Amalaka remembered as well.

The past coming back to her, as it hadn't for years and years, saw tears coming down her own face.

Holding the girl to her she said soothingly, “I will help you find your people. I promise.”

The girl continued to cry, but Amalaka picked up a grape. Holding it to the girl's lips she said, “You must eat. You must be strong. The future is yours.”

The girl looked at her and then took the grape. Gazing up at her she whispered, “What good is the future, when I cannot remember the past?”

“It does not matter what you can remember or can't remember. You exist, and because you do, there is hope.”

The girl ate and Amalaka continued to hold her, as she pondered on the events of this day.

The artificial inseminations had stopped ten years ago.

It had been made clear that there was to be no continual propping up of the female population, even as the war against them by the machines had increased dramatically. There had been little positive to find in life before this moment, but now with the advent of this child, everything had changed.

This girl existed, and she had even confessed to having a father. Where there was one, there might be more. Perhaps at last, at long last, things would start to go back to the way they had once been.

Oh, how to God she had prayed for that very thing during the bitterly long years of her life. Now, as she held this girl, it was like a dream come true.

The girl trustingly continued to eat while sitting in her lap, even as Amalaka had the emotions swell within her of her most cherished wish, that had been denied to her all her life. For the first time, she felt like a mother.

She wasn't the girl's mother, but she would play the part of one. Even if it came down to the loss of her own life, she would see to it that this girl had a future.

Knowing the many harsh realities of continued existence though, she whispered out, “God, please help me!”

The girl looked up and innocently asked, “Who is God?”

Amalaka smiled gently. “I think you already know Him, but until you remember, I will tell you of who He is.”

CHAPTER TWO

Responsibility Taken

The Next Day

The morning air rang with the sound of hammer strikes. It was not the usual rhythm or even close to the volume of sound that was typical to be heard from the smithy. A young apprentice was learning.

Inside the shop, Amalaka had to bite back a smile. The little girl was swinging the smallest hammer in her collection, with the utmost determination, as she pounded away at the end of the glowing red-hot metal ingot, which she held out over the anvil for the girl to pound upon.

The girl was ruining it, but that was okay. She was learning.

Add to that she was also trying her very best to replicate the style that she had been witnessing in Amalaka's work. Amalaka didn't mind the desecration taking place at all, given those realities.

Instead, she encouraged the girl. When she thought the girl wouldn't be crushed by it, she let her know some of the things that she was doing wrong. The girl nodded and did her best to follow instruction.

It was endearing, even as it was heartwarming to see someone so dedicated to getting something just right. It reminded her of herself in some ways.

She was so engrossed in the girl's progress that she didn't notice Salantha, the self-termed leader of the colony, until much later than would have been usual for her to. Such oversights could be costly.

Amalaka quickly stilled the girl's next drawn back hammer strike. The girl looked up questioningly and Amalaka said, "That is good for now, Ayayla. Go and wash up."

The girl noticed the other woman standing off to the side and jumped back, completely startled. Amalaka could understand why.

Salantha would have once been termed as a very beautiful woman, but now one half of her face was marred by three deep scars that drug down from her forehead all the way to her jawline. How she still had her eye, given the path of the middle scar, was a wonder as it passed directly overtop of it.

The girl, as if sensing the danger this other woman could represent, quickly set down the little hammer and ran off to disappear elsewhere.

Amalaka calmly set the misshapen piece of iron aside. Letting her gaze rise, she met Salantha's.

Salantha inclined her head after the girl and asked softly, "Is that her name?"

"She cannot remember her name, so I have given her a new one."

"I've never heard it before."

"It comes from a very long time ago in a different language than the one we speak today."

Salantha gave a nod and then said, "I would like you to walk with me."

Amalaka nodded.

The two women headed out of the smithy. There had always been a live let live relationship between these two women in the ten years since Amalaka had changed her smithy location to reside in this colony.

Truly her presence here had only benefited the colony and Salantha's rule, but in the world they lived in, things could change rapidly.

Salantha wasted no time, "The girl is young. Too young."

Amalaka nodded.

"Why is that?" the other woman knowingly baited.

"You know why. There is at least one man out there, somewhere."

Salantha stopped walking. The two women looked out over the vast plain before them that many animals grazed upon.

Amalaka didn't know what to make of the other woman's silence. A little girl's life was held in the balance.

Quietly, she prayed for direction to the Creator of all that was before her, even as she had prepared herself to kill the other woman standing beside her - and any other that lifted a finger against the girl. She couldn't kill them all, but she could take out some of them.

Salantha would be the hardest. She was very fast and very skilled.

Salantha's gaze came to her knowingly. She looked away again and the two of them watched in the distance as a lion pride went about taking down a cow of mixed origin.

Domestic cows had interbred with water buffalo and the grassland before them was a shifting array of colors as not seen in the past, but one that was now natural for their gazes to look upon.

Salantha spoke, "What are your plans for her?"

"To raise her as my own."

"And?"

"Get her the hell away from what so many of the others have become."

Salantha's gaze came to hers challengingly.

Her tone clipped she asked, "Am I one of those '*others*' you speak of?"

"Are you?" Amalaka stated back, equally challenging in response.

The two women's eyes did war for a long moment.

Salantha looked away.

The lions were feeding now. Softly she said, "I hope not."

Amalaka blinked.

Cautiously she said, as she felt led somehow from within to do it, "There might be others like her. Out there somewhere. We should find them. Bring them here. Protect them."

A sudden disturbance directed Amalaka's attention to a large party of riders coming from the colony towards them.

"Already ahead of you on that one, old one."

Amalaka looked back to her. Testing the bounds of their relationship further than she ever had she whispered, "If you find more children, I ask that you would bring them to me. Please."

Amalaka had never shown so much weakness before and Salantha gazed at her now curiously. She gave a slight nod of the head in answer to the other's plea.

The riders were drawing close.

"Amalaka, please do not give out any more of your weapons to fools. The one has almost cut her arm off and another has already lost her sword. You could have come to me and I would have given you the girl."

"I couldn't take that risk."

Salantha regarded her somberly.

Before the riders drew too close to hear she asked, "What do you think it all means?"

Amalaka knew she meant the girl's young age as having obviously been the result of being sired by an actual male.

Amalaka gave her the truth, as she had come to see it during the past few days. "The end is near. If men have truly survived, our enemies will come for us like never before."

Salantha nodded, as the riders drew up. "I think you are right." she said, suddenly looking very weighed down by the role of leadership.

Going to her horse, she mounted up. Before she could ride off Amalaka asked, "Why then would you not kill her, out of fear of the change that she will bring?"

Salantha gazed down at her steadily. With frankness she said, "I am tired of living in fear. Aren't you?"

She didn't wait for an answer, but turned her horse in the direction of where the girl had been found in the forests off to the east.

Amalaka watched her go until they were almost out of sight, all the while silently praising her Maker for what seemed like a sudden change of heart on the part of at least some within the colony. For once she did not feel so utterly alone in spirit.

A little hand slipped into hers. Glancing down, she beheld the little girl, who truly had taken to her as a mother figure. For the first time in a very long time, there was hope.

There was also the chance - more than ever - of complete annihilation.

CHAPTER THREE

Tears & Ashes

The singing trill of forest songbirds was steady in its rhythm, but Salantha was not deceived. The Borgs often replicated natural sounds for the sole purpose of allaying fears in those that were being hunted.

Their replication ability of nature was almost perfect; however, no matter how precise the actual birdcall was duplicated, there was to the trained ear a slight echo not present in the call of nature's creatures.

Many would have been deceived, though, by the replication. Truly, many already had been.

The calls that she now heard echoing through the forest were just that. Far too much echo.

They had left the horses behind, and now with the grace of sleek cats, the scouting party of women stole quietly down a game trail. Deer and other forest dwellers grazed peacefully here and there in the sun dappled understory vegetation.

The Borgs did not hunt them. Only humans were their targets of interest.

What the women were currently about was sheer insanity. One should always make a run for it, if the knowledge of a Borg in the area was so obvious to be had as it was.

One simply did not go onwards toward them. And one certainly did not try to hunt them.

It was too risky, with the possibility of death or severe injury being an almost certain possibility. That said, running from them often bore the same results.

Once there had been no need to run, unless one was too old to bear children. Salantha remembered only too well of how in the past she had been caught, stung by electric charge, and then been forcibly inseminated by something not even human.

She'd borne two children to life. Both were now dead.

Now at thirty-eight years of age she was one of the oldest women she knew. If things were as they had been and she was caught again, she would have likely been executed.

Essentially, the Borgs just turned up the electric charge, until you literally burned up from the inside. Now, however, there was no hope for even the younger women, as the Borgs just killed everyone now.

No one had been forcibly impregnated with female offspring only, in at least ten years. The girl back at the colony was special.

Her creation could be the key to everything. That was the only reason she was risking the lives of everyone right now on this perilous excursion.

If something didn't change in the way of things soon, they'd all be dead, no matter how well they fought or hid. No new girls meant no new life.

The few that survived the genocide would grow old and die childless. The writing was on the wall. Because of that, such missions as this were a necessity.

The repetitive echo of the all-too-real sounding songbirds was growing fainter. Somehow they had managed to slip through, but that was no guarantee that there weren't more Borgs lurking about on silent mode.

Reaching a cul-de-sac, Salantha eased into it and let herself lean back against the sidewall of it. She breathed heavily for a moment as the twenty-odd other women with her filed into the depression. They all leaned back tiredly to breathe, with the same heavy laden hysteria that each felt.

Everyone's eyes were wide with fright and adrenaline. Even though their breathing was heavy, they did it with much reserve, trying not to be overly loud, lest they be heard.

No one dared to speak aloud.

Salantha wondered how many of them wished to return to the horses, but to her surprise as she read the sign language taking place amongst them, there was no one saying that. It was another odd occurrence.

Everyone was in unity for once, even though the likelihood of a painful death was extremely high at the present. Eavesdropping in, she read the report that there were three Borgs on songbird lullaby, one acting as a crow and at least one on silent killer mode.

One woman had seen the silent Borg that had made no call. There were most likely a few more silent mode ones in the vicinity.

The reality of five or more Borgs all in the same area was highly unusual. Usually there were no more than two in a sector of forest this large.

Why were there so many?

The answer was clear. They had perceived an unparalleled threat, and now they were actively hunting it to an extreme measure, that had resulted in this over compensation.

Were men really that much of a danger to them? If so, then she wanted one.

Anything that could make the Borgs go overboard like this was to be capitalized on. If she hadn't seen a few tattered pictures as a girl, she wouldn't even know what the other half of her own species looked like.

Her grandmother was the last of her lineage to have seen an actual man, and it was only her great-grandmother who had actually been mated to one.

It was that endangered quality of reality that made Amalaka so interesting. She'd never pressed, but it had always been clear to her that the older woman was hiding a past that none of them could boast of.

To a one, they were all the offspring brought about by the assault of an inhuman entity forcing a stunned woman down into the mud somewhere. If the stories about men were true, the reality of being with them was little better at times, but then there were the other stories.

The legends that talked about love, and even pleasure. Without a man to witness, however, it appeared they were just stories.

That indeed was why they were here. They were in search of the legend.

Nerves somewhat more in check now, Salantha eased out of the depression and moved on, silently followed by the others. She felt very grateful that no one was questioning her leadership decisions right now, especially her choice to go onward in this perilous quest.

It seemed that their desire for a change in the status quo was as great as hers was.

Creeping along a game trail, Salantha abruptly froze in place. Everyone did.

Salantha made a hand signal, and as one the women melted off to the sides and virtually disappeared from sight. They had become very adept at hiding.

If you didn't hide, you died.

In the distance there was the stamp of steady repercussions that vibrated through the ground. The vibration got louder by the second, until they were all viewing what was making it.

The lumbering approach of a Borg on the trail coming from the direction they had been headed in.

It was one of the older models, not that there were any that you could exactly call new, but this one was older than most. The grind of gears and the resistant creak of metal-on-metal was loud, and yet the hunk of beaten up old junk continued to operate.

Continued to kill, the sight of a splash of red across the Borg's chest plate being clear evidence to the reality that something had died.

Had it been a man? How she desperately hoped not.

None of the women moved as the thing continued to tramp away too loudly in order to maintain operational secrecy. Then the ground vibrated even more, in the direction of the other Borgs that the women had slipped past. There came the sudden knowledge that the Borgs were all moving out.

Their work here was done apparently. The forest was now utterly silent in the wake of their passage from it.

Several long moments passed as no one dared to breathe. Only when she could feel no more vibrations did Salantha creep back out to the trail. The others followed her more slowly.

Not one of them had ever experienced such an encounter as this. The threat level of being here was hardly diminished with the retreat of the Borgs.

There were other predators about - besides the Borgs that were big enough to prey on women. However, there was also safety in numbers to an extent.

The natural sounds of the forest remained muted. A sense of foreboding built up within Salantha, but it was not in relation to imminent danger.

It was the unshakable feeling that they were too late.

Salantha saw a rise of smoke coming from nearby. Leaving the trail, she and the others crept through the understory, virtually soundless.

There in a small clearing lay a Borg. It was permanently out of commission.

Then with a gasp a woman pointed. Beyond the first Borg lay another.

Two Borgs!

Over the years they had taken their fair share of the things out, but never two at once.

Sensing the coast was clear, Salantha went out to confirm that the first one and then the second were entirely done for. It was always best to make sure, as sometimes they played dead.

Clear evidence of their having been in a battle was to be attested to. Salantha saw the body then.

It was a woman. Her skin was like that of Amalaka's.

She was dead. Suddenly unmindful of being found by the Borgs, Salantha stood up and came closer to the woman.

She'd been run through by a Borg blade. She hadn't died instantly.

She lay half on her side, with her head turned looking off to the side, even as one hand was outstretched in that direction. The woman had been very pretty.

Not just naturally pretty, but it was like she had intentionally taken the time to care for her appearance in order to be viewed as pretty. Her eyes were still open and told the story of an emotion that was only definable as extreme loss.

Salantha stopped to gaze down at the woman, as had the others. The woman on the ground wore a dress, and she had a flower in her hair, along with several items of jewelry. None of those standing about her could boast the same adornment.

None of them had ever had a reason to want to improve their looks. To look nice.

What was the point?

Then as one, the group turned and started to move with leadened feet toward a charred black spot on the forest floor not far away. Seeming distant from her own senses, Salantha felt the impact of her knees connecting with the ground.

Her vision was obscured by sudden tears. As she tried to blink them away, she took note of the wail that had risen up out of her own throat. She was not alone.

The others were as she was. They would have all been easily picked off by a single Borg just then.

Somehow that didn't matter, as they were all too heartbroken to care about continued life. Her body shaking with broken-hearted cries that were hard to explain, Salantha let her hand fall down to the charred ground, where only the ashes of what they all knew had once been a man, remained.

He was no more now. Gone, forever.

Jerking on sobs, Salantha turned her head to view the fallen woman, whose eyes seemed to be gazing right through her and on towards the spot of charred ground, whereon lay the outline of a body now burned to nothing but ash.

Salantha closed her eyes and only sobbed all the louder. The legends were true.

Love, the kind talked about, between a man and a woman, was real. Even in death, the expression of anguish at seeing the loss of the one you loved was undeniable.

An unbearable ache for what the woman had known formed within Salantha's middle, and she hugged herself tightly about with her arms. Opening her eyes, she stared up at the sky through the leaves of the silent trees.

She had no words to describe the way she felt for the loss of someone she had never met. In a way, it felt like the world had just died.

The hope was gone, all over again.

Crying out she said brokenly, "Oh, God....Please! I....I can't go on if...... what's the point of all this?"

They were not the words or scenes of emotional brokenness that a leader would ever want to release before those that they led; but in the moment, they were all in unison with her, even as they nodded their heads while tears dripped off their chins to splatter down into the ashes of a man.

Gaining her feet, even as her eyes continued to pour out grief she hadn't known she'd had stored away for such a moment as this, she pointed to the fallen woman. With a shaking finger she emotionally screamed out, "I want what she had! I..... are You even there? Do You care about us at all?"

Shouting as she weaved about on her feet, she gestured around. "We're all dead women. We... we are less than nothing. I.... just kill us and be done with this torture called living!

We only become less as we age. Haven't we paid enough! Hasn't there been enough pain! I.... kill me, and if You won't, I will. If I can't ever have what she had for even a moment, then I don't want one more day of this miserable life!"

Jerking a swipe of her arm across her eyes, she cleared them enough to focus on pulling the dagger out of her belt. She'd never been more serious in her life.

Bringing the blade up to her chest, she started to push.

"Do not dare to do it, Salantha. Not after you have challenged Me!"

Crying out with fright as she felt overcome from both within and without, she dropped the dagger and crashed down to grovel with her face on the ground, as her whole being shook. There wasn't a woman present who wasn't also stretched out flat in complete submission to the Voice that had been heard by them all.

Weeping like never before, it felt like she'd been caught up in a river of some unknown current. She clung to the ground with more terror than she'd ever known in her life.

"Peace."

Almost instantly, the sobs of the prostrate women ceased as they obeyed the command. Bodies still shaking, they lay as they were, not daring to even lift their heads.

It had suddenly become clear to them all that there actually was a God, and right now He was angry at them. There were worse things than simply dying.

"I am not angry. None of you knows enough of Me for me to fault you for much of anything. I pity you instead."

Cautiously the women lifted their heads, then cried out with renewed fear as all of them saw a vision of someone, outlined by rays of light, that had the form and appearance of the woman, whose physical body still lay upon the ground, sightlessly dead. As she stood quietly by her own body, her head remained lowered, as if she waited for permission of some kind.

The Voice that shook their souls and seemed like it should have consumed the forest with its glory said, **"Speak to them. Tell them your story."**

The white light outlined vision that must be the woman's spirit lifted her head and smiled softly down at them.

"I was once as you are. I cried out as you have, Salantha. God heard me and He took away my reproach. We deserve destruction for our actions, truly. We and our mothers before us have no excuse. We don't deserve Grace, but He gave it to me anyway. It is not a man that you are all crying over right now, that you need the most in your lives. You need a relationship with your Heavenly Father, first and foremost. Then, when you have that, He will give you what you have need of. He is faithful, just, and true. I may now not be of this life, but I am not without life. You have one among you who cares now for my daughter. She knows of the God I serve. She knows how to lead you all to the Saving Grace I received, but that comes with belief through only One Man, the Creator's Son. She will tell you about this Man, and how He saved everyone on Earth by what He did a very long time ago now. All memory of this Risen Savior may be lost to you in this moment, but Amalaka remembers. I implore you all to listen to her. May God's Grace come to you and reside in you, even as it did in me, and will now for forever."

The light of her countenance dimmed for a second, seeming to ask a question not of the women on the ground, but rather of the Voice of authority whose Spirit lay so heavy about the place as to say that it had somehow become hallowed ground. She asked, "May I ask something of You before I leave this place, Father?"

"You may."

"I would ask of you that these women, who have cried over the remains of something that they have never seen, would be granted a reprieve by You. I ask that they would be given a man of their own and the experience of their own children with that man, even as You were so gracious as to give that life to me?"

"It delights Me to hear words such as yours, daughter, given on the behalf of others. It speaks of the love I found in your heart and reminds Me why I sacrificed My own Son for one such as you, who has come through the fire to be with Me, now and for forever. So let it be as you have asked for these strangers to you, for it is not too hard a thing for Me to do. Yes indeed, I am willing to see it done. Not one who has cried this day in brokenness of spirit will age even a day, until the time of their reproach be lifted away."

The women sobbed all the louder at the words of majesty spoken over them, as even now it felt like those selfsame words were entering into them, changing something from within.

Salantha lifted her head to see the spirit of the woman fading away from view.

Gazing down at her softly the woman's spirit said, "Watch over my girl for me."

Salantha, still crying, nodded her head with promise. The spirit of the woman disappeared from view, and the presence of what felt like all power and might went away in part, but in some ways it seemed to remain in them still.

There was so much that they didn't know!

The urge to return and speak with Amalaka was suddenly at the forefront of all their minds. They wanted to know more.

Wiping at her eyes, Salantha spoke aloud. "Before we go, we will bury them together. I think that is how it used to be done."

The other women nodded emotionally, then working together as one they started digging a grave with their weapons. They laid the body of the woman in the grave. Then each of them began to scoop up the ashes of the man and put them with the woman, who had interceded for them in order that they might experience what she had.

They wetted the ground with their tears as they closed the Earthly remains of the couple over with the soil of the ground.

CHAPTER FOUR

A Name Claimed

Amalaka looked up from the glowing steel as she saw Ayayla dart past. The child could move like the wind.

Concerned, she set the blade to the side and made to follow. She was still concerned for Ayayla's safety within the colony.

Clearing the doorway, it was to see Ayayla standing out in the open, staring out toward the open plain. Amalaka felt a stirring of irritation within her, for Ayayla had gone out too far from the smithy.

Her hearing was not what it used to be, and if something were to happen she might not hear it in time. Her lips opened, but then abruptly shut as a voice from within said, **"Do not call out to her."**

Trembling, Amalaka started to kneel down, but once again the voice admonished, **"Do not kneel. I do not need that in order to see the condition of your heart. I see it clearly. It is clear that you both remember and have chosen to uphold the beliefs of your fathers. You are blessed for doing so, even as you have not allowed your heart to yet grow cold."**

Still trembling, even as tears spilled down her cheeks, Amalaka gruffly said, "How can you say such things? I have done things. Terrible things to survive. I....I turned my back on You for years. There's so much that I should have done. Could have done. I...."

"Amalaka."

Amalaka shut up.

Her lips quivering, she remained quiet.

"You yet remember authority. My authority. That is a great deal. As for love - what you have done for the child makes it so that I can overlook a great multitude of sins."

"Thank you, Lord," Amalaka whispered with both relief and shame.

"I'm not done with you. Soon you are going to be My mouthpiece to those who will listen. It is a great burden I am about to lay on you; and yet you are not without choice. Will you accept this burden I have for you to bear?"

Trembling, she nodded even as she whispered, "Yes, Lord."

"Despite whatever you believe of yourself, I tell you right now that your heart is right with Me. Now, the riders draw near. Go comfort the child. For not only have I burdened you with My commission, but I have made you the guardian of a young, precious life. You named her well. I will make her fast and as fleet of foot as any gazelle, even as I bless her with beauty of spirit. Her mother's and her father's faithful ways will never leave her, even as I will return to her the fruit of their dedication to me, after many days have passed."

Shaking both inwardly and outwardly, Amalaka went out of the blacksmith shop that, in truth, she had been hiding in for years and years on end.

No more.

Speaking to others had never been her thing, but she would do it. As God was finally at last once more her strength, she would do and say whatever He told her to, no matter the cost.

Coming to a stop, she remained behind Ayayla. Waiting with her, she let her eyes rise from the child to take in the approaching riders.

She blinked as she beheld a strange countenance upon them all. In fact, the change was so stark that it made her wonder if they were the same people who had ridden out just the day before.

Remorse was written in every line of their beings, even as they slumped dejectedly in their saddles as if they bore the weight of the world on their shoulders. They had all returned - what was the cause of this mournfulness of spirit?

Amalaka was further shocked when Salantha got down off her horse, only to fall to her knees. Then on her knees and hands, she crawled forward the rest of the distance to Ayayla.

It was both humbling and awful, the quality of remorse that there was about her.

Amalaka had never seen her cry, even when she had lost her last daughter to a hungry lion pride. A lion pride that she had then slain single-handedly.

No one had ever done anything like that. It was clear she had not expected to live, either.

Her marred face was a reminder of just how close she had come to death. She had always been a woman seemingly driven by a quiet fury, but now all Amalaka saw was brokenness and a heart that reflected tenderness, as she pulled out a pretty necklace from a pocket and gently set it around Ayayla's neck.

Amalaka was beyond overwhelmed by what she was seeing. Many of the colony had come to watch, and were as astonished as she was at what was taking place.

Under her breath Amalaka whispered, "What have you done, my God?"

"You will see."

Amalaka's eyes were drawn back to Ayayla as her small body gave a sharp jerk. She was holding in one hand the golden object that had the form of a deer to it.

She gave such a cry of misery then, that it broke Amalaka's heart. Salantha covered her own mouth with a hand reflexively, even as she made a motherly sounding shushing noise.

Then the little girl's arms were about Salantha's neck as she hugged her like she was drowning.

Amalaka drew close and Ayayla looked up.

Wailing she said, "I remember! I remember everything!"

Amalaka fell to her knees and enfolded both crying individuals in her arms, as they seemed to both need the comfort of it.

Amalaka did not know what had happened, but she could see that God was at work.

Salantha drew back a little. Addressing Ayayla, she said, "I..... I wish there was something I could give you of your father, but all..... all that remained was ash. We buried him with your mother. They loved each other very much, didn't they?"

Ayayla nodded her head vigorously, still sobbing.

Salantha pulled a small leather pouch out of a pocket. Looking unsure of herself she said, "I took some of your father's ashes and I put them in this bag. I know he is dead, but you are not alone. We will protect you. One day, when you have a man to call your own, that will be the day that it is time to bury this. Until that day, you will still have a part of your father with you."

Ayayla took the pouch from her and bent over it, seemingly inconsolable. Salantha look at her uncertainly and then to Amalaka.

Amalaka leaned forward and kissed Salantha's forehead. Then meeting her tearful gaze she said, "I am proud of you. You have done well."

That said, she scooped Ayayla up and held her to herself tightly. She'd never been blessed to be a mother - that is, until now.

The responsibility threatened to break her heart, as all she wanted to do was take away all the pain. She couldn't though; but just the same, she tried.

Opening her eyes, she was witness to the reality of all of the riders on their knees in the dust. Brokenly they whispered in almost perfect harmony, "Please, Amalaka, tell us of the God we know that you serve! Please! He said you would show us the way."

Nodding emotionally, Amalaka said, "I will tell you all I know, and I have a book of His words, too. I…I should have shared it with you a long time ago. I am sorry. I will tell you all I know, I promise. but first let me comfort the child."

To a one they nodded and moved off, until it was only Amalaka, Ayayla, and Salantha.

Salantha spoke, "I will not let anything happen to her. I promise it on my life."

Smiling emotionally, Amalaka reached out with a free hand to trace it down over what would have been a perfectly formed face, if it weren't for the scars that marred half of it.

"I know you will. You were a good mother, Salantha. I never told you that, but I should have. I didn't comfort you when you lost your last child. I am sorry for my silence. I…"

Salantha's hand closed over her lips to keep her from speaking further. Staring into the older woman's eyes she said, "I forgive you. Please, I have so much that I am in need of forgiveness for, don't burden yourself with what you have or haven't done."

Amalaka nodded. For a moment her eyes closed, and then they opened. Regarding Salantha perceptively, she said, "You will have a child yet."

Salantha nodded, even as she whispered, "All of us who went will. The Voice….." Salantha pointed upward hesitantly, ".....He said it would be so."

Smiling even as she continued to hold Ayayla to her, Amalaka said, "You will have a son."

That was simply too much for Salantha. Taking her hand away from her own lips she puzzled out loud. "I know what was said, but surely I will be too old. He said we would not age, but how can that be so?"

"No, this you must learn about the Creator we both now serve. What He says He will do, even that He truly will do, even as He is not a liar. You will have a child and it will be a son."

Salantha breathed out, "I will have a son," as if she couldn't believe it, but somehow did anyway.

"I don't even know what a boy looks like."

Amalaka chuckled, "Before you do, you first must see what a man looks like."

Salantha's face flushed red, but the attention of both women was drawn to Ayayla, who turned from hiding her face against Amalaka.

Clutching at the bag of ashes with one hand, even as the other lay clasped over the golden deer on the necklace, she met Salantha's concerned gaze and whispered, "Thank you. I will do as you have said."

Amalaka gently asked, "You remember your name now, from before?"

The girl nodded, but then said, "I liked it, but my new name is Ayayla, even as you gave it to me when I had nothing. I will respect that name as mine from this day forward."

Both women glanced at each other as they thought in unison, *'What child spoke like this?'*

The only answer was - this child. This child was truly special.

Amalaka clutched her a little tighter to her, even as Salantha soothingly brushed the girl's wild hair out of her face.

Neither woman, since the advent of this child, was acting at all as she had before in life up until now. It was like a new day had begun, and they had both chosen to embrace it for all they were worth.

CHAPTER FIVE

Safe in the Night

Wearily, Amalaka closed the old Bible that she had somehow managed to hold on to through the years of upheaval. In a way, it was all she had left of her father.

She had thought Ayayla was asleep, and was surprised when the girl spoke. "I remember that story. My father told it to me."

Amalaka let her hands move over the riotous abandon of curls on the girl's head. It was nice to know that the tradition she had experienced had continued.

It was also good to know that there must be more old Bibles out there.

It had been hard to accurately translate the Bible into the language the others spoke, which was really a mash-up of various languages all rolled into one, but she had tried. Despite the difficulty in translating, she thought she had done rather well.

Many were silently gathered about the fire. Not everyone, but many.

Many had come. As one they all seemed to be quietly staring into the flame reflectively.

Silently, Amalaka prayed for them as she coaxingly worked her fingers lovingly through the girl's head of thick hair that lay on her leg.

She could read from the Bible until she was blue in the face, and yet it would do no good, unless the Spirit of God called. Thankfully it was obvious to her eyes and spirit that God's set-apart Spirit was calling.

She could never have imagined such a thing possible. She had thought these women, indeed even herself, lost to the barbarism seemingly demanded by continued survival in a world that was harsh and uncertain, even at the best of times.

She had been wrong. So wrong.

She felt tears coursing down her face.

A hand nearby reached out and squeezed her shoulder consolingly. It was a young woman she recognized, who had recently brought her a sizeable amount of trade goods in order to secure for herself one of her blades.

Amalaka had accepted the commission, inwardly surprised that one so young could have amassed so much wealth. Young as she was though, she had already become one of Salantha's most trusted allies in the colony.

Her long blonde hair lay braided as it curved gracefully over her shoulder. Despite the general lack of adornment present among the women, Amalaka had noticed that this woman did more than most to appear feminine.

She was yet warrior enough, though, to keep the advances of the more masculine types pushed back. It was those given over to playing the role of a male the most, that had not come here tonight.

They seemingly had no interest in this change that was occurring, which did not surprise Amalaka, as it was almost biblical for them to be distanced from the truth, because of their errant desires.

The blonde's name was Sytana. Without words she clearly conveyed her gratitude to Amalaka for sharing the words of the Bible with them.

Shaking her head Amalaka brokenly whispered, "I am so sorry that..... that I have waited so long. Please, I beg forgiveness of you, all of you."

Many nodded, some murmured their thanks, but Sytana whispered, "You're forgiven."

Amalaka nodded emotionally, even as more consoling hands reached out in the semi-darkness to touch her briefly.

Speaking loud enough to be heard by all, she continued. "I will come here every night and read more from God's words. If any of you have questions, you are welcome to come to me at any time of the day, and I will put aside my work and do my best to answer them. You have my word on this."

Gratitude was evident on the faces of many, but in the semi-darkness it was Sytana that Amalaka focused in on. The girl looked bound up with anxiousness to ask a question.

Reaching forward Amalaka squeezed the blonde's knee and asked earnestly, "What is it you want to ask?"

The girl blushed, royally bushed. Face red, she murmured something too low to hear.

For such a superlative warrior in combat, she was very shy in this exposed social gathering. Amicably Amalaka said, "Relax, girl, but do speak louder. We are all dying to know what it is you want to know."

Many were smiling, and well aware of having everyone's attention, the blushing blond managed to choke out, "We know you are old. Far older than any of us. Did you...... have you...... I mean......" The girl's face was in flames.

She was curious; they all were. Gently, Amalaka squeezed the girl's knee again before removing her hand.

Meeting her eyes she said, "No, I have not been with a man."

Though embarrassed through and through, Amalaka did not miss the look of disappointment that clouded the girl's youthful and very beautiful face.

"However, when I was a girl, I once came upon my father and mother being made one flesh."

The girl looked back up instantly.

Amalaka glanced around the group gathered about the fire and said, "It is nothing at all like what many of us have experienced at the hands of the Borgs. Nothing like that at all. While I suppose it could be like what we see within the animals around us, all I can say is that for my father and mother it was not like that. They were passionate for each other and yet they were not animals. They..... were loving with one another. Passionate too, but very loving. They both enjoyed being made as one flesh together. I..... even as young as I was, I knew..... that was what I wanted - what they had - but...... well, I am old now and past my time. But you, Sytana, you will know the joy that my mother had. It is so much more than simply just the joining of physical bodies together. So much more than that."

The blonde looked down at her hands that were trembling as they gripped each other in her lap. She had been one of those to accompany Salantha.

"Speak child. Others need to hear what it is you have to say," Amalaka encouraged.

Sytana looked back up with tears in her eyes. "I feel different inside."

Many murmured in agreement from the shadows.

"How?" Amalaka gently encouraged her to elaborate.

In all of her life she had never been so gentle with others as she had the past few days, but now it seemed like it was what her spirit was made of.

All she wanted to do was give to others.

The blond spoke. "I....I don't even know why, but I..... I feel him. At least, I think so. I can't see him, but I have this feeling in my mind that I'm....... that I'm no longer alone. It's...... it's the best feeling of my life!"

Amalaka nodded to encourage the young woman, even as other women were nodding as tears dripped off their chins.

Her voice quivering with emotion, Sytana said, "I want to go to him. I mean...... literally, right now, I would get up and go out into the dark just to be with him. I ache. I don't even know what he looks like, but I want everything! I will give him everything! I will!" the girl declared, as if challenging any to doubt her fervency of spirit.

"I believe you, child," Amalaka said affirmingly.

Pain seemed to be rawly expressed now in the girl's eyes, and then her voice as she said, "But I don't know where he is! I..... I have this fear that..... that I'm just dreaming. That what I want will never happen, and indeed why should it? You read to us for hours from the words of a Creator I knew had to exist, but knew nothing about other than what I can see. What I can see of us is that....... is that we are shameful. We are not right! I don't want this life. I would sooner die than continue in this life, if I knew I couldn't have what I have dreamed of. I know it's wrong, but I want the life I have dreamed of more than this air I breathe right now."

"Not wrong, Sytana. Not wrong," Amalaka encouraged.

The girl looked at her as if not believing her words.

"You were there in the forest, Sytana. You remember what happened to us," Salantha said, speaking up for the first time.

The girl shivered with remembrance.

"Trust that. If you can't bring yourself to believe another's words, just trust that experience you had, because you know it was real what happened to us. You know it, Sytana!"

The girl nodded emotionally.

Salantha gentled her tone. "He is real. You will find him. You will bear his children."

Sytana nodded shakily, as she visibly fought to find faith in a future that truly would be a dream come true for her.

Her mouth twisting with a quirky smile, Salantha said, "You may not know what he looks like, but I bet you he will like what you look like."

The girl flushed again, even as it was evident that she knew it was the truth; as if it was some kind of proverbial truth that she'd been made to appear attractive to a male she'd never seen, by a Creator that had ordained for such things to be.

Suddenly serious, Salantha said, "You are yet a virgin, are you not?"

Sytana's face was beyond red now, but she nodded dutifully in answer.

"See that you remain so for him. That goes the same for any of you others that can say the same. I feel that is an important way to be for a man, your man. At least, I feel inside like it is so."

Her gaze went to Amalaka, who nodded and affirmed, "It is very important. It says so in God's words. You have sensed the truth before even truly knowing it, Salantha."

Salantha looked down.

Amalaka addressed the group in general. "It is not good what we as women have done with each other without the presence of a man among us. As you value a future that sees us once more united with the other half of our kind, I ask you to stop those former behaviors. It is not the way of the Creator for women to be with women, any more than it is for men to be with men. Yes, that did happen, and I believe it is one of the main reasons men were destroyed. If we do not want to repeat the mistakes of the past, then we need to stop doing what is wrong in the present.

"One thing I do know of God, is that we cannot have things our way and also His way at the same time. He doesn't want half of everything from those who believe in Him. He wants everything. We please Him before we do anything for ourselves. He will reward those who seek Him. He will, for He said so in the Bible. I believe it now as never before."

Silence reigned then around the fire. It was now late in the night.

What she had just asked was a lot for some of those gathered to entertain, and yet no one had left. Then, as the women remained by the fire, unoffended by what she had asked of them, a curious thing happened.

Almost together as one, the women lay down on the ground right where they were and fell asleep. Everyone, that was, except for Amalaka.

Eyes wide, she stared about wondering what was wrong. However, what could be wrong when everything felt so right in her spirit.

But still?

Worried, she glanced from Salantha to Sytana and then others. Deep even breaths for air continued to raise the chest of each with evidence of continued life.

Even Ayayla was fast asleep. Still concerned though, Amalaka started to lean over to shake Salantha; but a voice from the shadows spoke, "Peace, Amalaka."

Amalaka abruptly jerked, but remained sitting as a robed figure of what appeared to be a man drew near and sat down across the fire from her, in the only openly available spot left.

All around him lay the bodies of some thirty or so women, completely passed out into unconsciousness. They were totally vulnerable to an attack of any kind.

No one ever slept out in the open like this!

"They're under no threat. My Master has reserved these women to His own will. By their choice to remain, they have unlocked this promise that I now give you. No beasts of the field or any creature of God's, set in its order of creation, will attack them in any way. Instead they will be your allies, even as The Great I Am has chosen to restore order once more upon the lands of Earth.

"Tomorrow, one of your number will have proof of this and she will share it with the rest. The faith of many will be strengthened. Also, those who did not come tonight have been cast out. Even now my Master has caused an evil spirit to move upon them. Even now they are leaving, and they will not be back. Any who fail to follow the words of wisdom you have imparted to those gathered will join their number, and likewise share in their damnation."

The figure across the fire arose then. He gestured outwardly. Amalaka's shaken gaze took in briefly the illuminated outlines of others in the dark, like the one by the fire, before all was once again too dark to see.

They were quite safe it would seem. Amalaka breathed easier with knowing that.

Indeed she had never felt such security of person as she did now. Quickly before the messenger of the Most High could disappear, she stumbled out with, "I….. how did…..I…."

"You did well. Continue reading to them, and my Master's set-apart Spirit will do the rest."

Amalaka nodded, and then gave a start of fear as the messenger came around the fire, ever mindful of not stepping on the bodies of the sprawled out women. Amalaka was already shaking when his hands came to her.

Gently he eased her backward down to the ground, even as he said, "Now it is time for you to dream of reunitement as well."

Amalaka's eyes blinked sleepily as she fought to not go under into the enveloping peace of something that promised fantasy.

"But I'm old," she heard herself murmur.

"So you are, but that is of little consequence for the Creator. You will see."

"How?" Amalaka whispered from what felt like a long distance away.

"Just believe."

Amalaka's eyes closed as her mind was invited into a special place, a place apart from the world she knew. A place where anything seemed possible.

The guardian messenger stood back up and remained as a sentinel in the light given off by the fire. A fire that did not diminish in heat or flame through the long hours of the night, even though no new wood was added to it.

CHAPTER SIX

Scars

Salantha walked briskly out into the surrounding plain. It was likely too late in the day to successfully come upon prey and get close enough in order to give the felling blow, but still she must try.

There was no food back at the colony. There was little else as well.

The others had left in the night. In some ways that was a relief, as the confrontation Salantha had been fearing would take place had now been averted without bloodshed.

What was not a relief; however, was that they were without food, because the pigs had taken it all with them.

Angrily, Salantha brushed at an errant strand of hair that had fallen across her eyes. If only she had not fallen asleep by the fire like that!

As much as she wanted to rail at herself though, there was no getting around the fact that she had just had the best night's rest of her life. It had been full of imagery, but she couldn't remember anything about it now.

How she wished that she could though.

Her stomach growled painfully. She came to a stop as she placed a hand to her stomach.

Hunger she had known many times, and yet as insistent as the urge was it did not consume her, in the way it usually did, to do whatever it took to assuage it away.

In fact today, despite the troubles of the thieves in the night, was so peaceful that the desire to just sit down in the grass and listen to the meadowlarks singing was a real temptation. Alas, she had others depending on her to help feed them.

She opened her eyes and abruptly started so badly that she almost fell backward. There, sitting but feet before her, was a full grown lioness.

The lioness was huge.

Inwardly quaking at the reality of what extreme danger she was in, Salantha despaired of continued life in that moment.

Her shaking hand fell to her sword handle. There was no way she could pull it free in time.

Why had the lioness not already slain her?

Looking up at her, she saw the beast's eyes seem to suddenly reflect remorse. Was such a thing possible?

Was the cat playing with her before the kill?

The big cat's head lowered, and then startled, Salantha watched it inch forward on its belly, until its head was at her feet and she could feel its heavy breath upon her legs. It made no move to look up.

It would have been a thing of ease to draw out her sword and slice its head free in its present position. Instead of doing so, Salantha's shaking hand fell free of the sword handle. Scarcely breathing, she slowly knelt down.

"What are you doing?" she whispered to the lioness.

Before she could properly react, the lioness's head came up; and yet instead of biting her head off, all the big cat did was to press its forehead against hers. There was such a wealth of emotion to be felt in this one-of-a-kind connection with a wild beast that it had tears quickly coming down her face.

Shaking with the emotion of memories, she realized who this lioness was. After her daughter had been slain and eaten, she had enacted a terrible vengeance upon the pride of lions responsible.

She had killed all of them, except for one. There had been one little cub shaking in the bushes. Not even in the war wrath she had been consumed by had she been able to bring herself to slay the innocent looking little cub.

This must be her, all grown up now.

"I'm so sorry! I took everything. I…." A big tongue was licking at the tears upon the scarred portion of her face.

Salantha's eyes opened and she stared directly into the lioness' eyes. It may have been an animal, but it was far from dumb.

The steady light of intelligence and memory was there to be gleaned. There was also a sense of forgiveness.

Salantha reached out and hugged her arms around the big cat's neck and cried. In some ways it seemed like the pain of the past had finally been resolved.

She could move on now. She would move on.

Her eyes opened again. Alarmed, she beheld not just one lion, but a whole pride of them. Startled she got up to her feet, but to a one they all regarded her somberly with no hint of aggression.

Not knowing what to do in this otherworldly moment Salantha asked, "What do you want from me?"

Their eyes blinked as if to say '*nothing*' in reply.

Salantha heard a noise then. She turned to see a huge alpha male headed her way.

He was dragging a large buck. He made the task look effortless.

He brought his kill up to her and dropped his biting hold upon it. She was so dead, if he wanted her to be so.

It was evident though that he did not wish for it. The lioness left her side to press her head lovingly in against the big male's mane.

He licked her head briefly, but maintained focus on Salantha.

Salantha glanced from him to back the way she had come. Finding her voice she asked timidly, "I don't suppose you could drag that a little farther, could you?"

Eyes widening, Salantha stepped back as the big male reclaimed his bite and started off in the direction of the colony, soon helped by several of the others.

The lioness, however, remained by her side the whole way back to the colony. If there had been any doubt in Salantha's heart before, it was now gone.

Irrevocably and forever gone.

~~~~~~~~~

Reaching the colony, Salantha did not have to convince anyone to restrain from attacking the lions that had killed quite a few women over the years. To a one, all were spellbound by the act of provision being made for them.

It only became more so as a pack of excited wolves drug in not one, but two deer into the colony surroundings. The lions looked at them disdainfully, as if not liking that they had been outdone.

The big male gave a chesty roar and left. His pride followed him, even as the large wolf pack made their exodus as well.

The big lioness remained by Salantha's side, though.

"You should go. You have a family once again. They need you. I.....I hope to have my own one day...... again. Now go, but come back whenever you like."

The big lioness pressed her head against her stomach briefly and then she was off, hurrying to catch up with the rest of the pride.

Salantha had the distinct feeling that she would be back.

A hand fell over her shoulder and squeezed. It was Amalaka.

She was smiling. Salantha had never seen the woman smile so much before.

"Come, let us give thanks and eat what God has provided us."
~~~~~~~~~

Salantha nodded and said, “Yes, let us do that.”

The two women turned to the three deer carcasses, even as a pack of jackals drug a gazelle in to add to the growing pile. They raced off with excited yips, as if happy to have done such a thing.

The women who had remained at the colony, and were now taking part in this blessing, were smiling even as their faces were awash with tears.

As they went about butchering the animals, there came the knowledge to each of them that there would be enough for everyone. Not only that, but that also there truly was a God; and He loved them enough to even manipulate the forces of nature to work in their favor.

CHAPTER SEVEN

Passed Over

Salantha smiled softly as the group settled down for a night of learning. Today they had done almost nothing.

Just eat and rest. No hunting forays or even patrols had been conducted.

If the other women were close by waiting to attack, she did not want the remaining number of women divided. Besides, since they had all the food they needed, the necessity of leaving the compound hadn't been a pressing one anyway.

Would the predators bring more tomorrow?

Whether they did or not, today had been an overwhelming act of merciful Grace.

Her ears twitched at a sudden rustle of movement in the dark.

Her hand went to her sword, only to still as she heard the rumble of a heavy, breath-laden pant. The lioness came in close to her, then abruptly plopped down directly at her back.

The heavy rumble of her purr was apparent. Nervously, the others closer to the fire gave each other smiles as they watched Salantha reach out and begin rubbing behind the ear of the lioness.

The heavy rumbling only grew more pronounced. Salantha felt the rest of them then.

The whole pride was here. Just out of sight in the darkness beyond the fire's light.

There would be no need of sentry duty tonight. The big male gave a husky roar from not far off.

Several of the women softly cried out with fear. It was a hard thing to accept how predator had suddenly become protector, but even so it was just so. Now it was serving as a witness of God's involvement in their lives, like no other witness could have.

Ayayla came forward toward her. Smiling, Salantha encouraged her to pet the big lioness. She did shyly, and then gasped as the lioness gave her a lick.

The lioness hooked a paw about the girl and dragged her in gently, until she lay sprawled out up against her side. Ayayla lay nestled back against the lion, even as the lioness let her foreleg droop protectively over the girl.

Ayayla's eyes were wide, but fear wasn't the strongest of the emotions present within them. Softly, she stroked the massive paw that lay over her, and the lioness seemed to drift off into sleep.

Salantha leaned forward and whispered, "I think she likes you. You put her to sleep."

Ayayla nodded her head excitedly, even as she looked very happy to be where she was, with a lioness for a protector. The security of the lions all about them felt as real as if there was a human army at watch.

Amalaka started to read from the Bible. All gathered eagerly listened, even as they all came to accept the presence of the lion pride that would not depart. Amalaka read for over three hours before she closed the book in her hand.

Having done little in the way of work today, the women were surprisingly, for the first time not tired, at least not like they had been last night, which none of them fully understood yet.

~~~~~~~~~

Amalaka, glancing around, decided to do something that was hard for her, even as being so openly available to interaction with others was unusual for her. She wasn't by nature a people person, but these women were no longer just people.

They were family. She could easily bring herself to do more for them.

Some of the women had started to drift off to sleep when Amalaka's words woke them right back to alertness. "My father was the last man that I know of anywhere to have existed. You see, back in those days, any surviving men left over from the Great War against the Signal - and the System behind it - were actively hunted down by the women of that day. For an entire generation before my mother was born, women had been hunting men.

"There were awards given out by the Borgs to successful hunters of men. It wasn't till the men were gone that the Borgs turned entirely insensitive in their handling of women. There were places for the women to go to in those days to be impregnated. It was not at that time the abuse that so many of you have had to suffer through.

"After the men were largely gone for several years, almost a decade, it became apparent that the women left alive had no desire for offspring.
~~~~~~~~~

The places set up for impregnation were shut down and the system of impregnation we have known for our whole lives, up till ten years ago, was implemented. It was in those days that my mother was running for her life, as the Borgs had not worked the glitches out of their new system yet.

"A lot of women were dying during the process of implantation, or being gravely injured by it. There was also just the difficulty one could expect in those days of being pregnant, as food was uncertain and strife almost constant. It was not a world to bring a child up in.

"A Borg caught my mother's trail. My mother made an all-out effort to escape. She was strong and fleet of foot. She almost got away, but in trying to escape she ran along the edge of a steep gully. She slipped and fell down into the gully, breaking her leg in the process.

"There she lay in the dust, with a badly broken leg, as the Borg came closer and closer to impregnate her. Her broken leg, though, was a death sentence for her, even if the process of impregnation hadn't been going to be one. The Borg would have deemed her unfit to carry offspring on account of her leg being broken. It was overtop of her and preparing to stun fry her to death, when instead of the feel of electricity, it was rather the sight of electric sparks shooting out everywhere from the Borg that occurred.

"The Borg turned from her, and that is when my mother saw my father for the first time. He had a spear with a special looking hardened alloy steel blade to it, and he was repeatedly stabbing it into the Borg. It swung at him repeatedly with its own blade and tried to fry him as well; but the man was able to block some of the attacks and was quick enough to evade the others. All the while though, he was actively penetrating the steel skin of the Borg, and eliminating systems.

"The Borg's actions now made erratic, ceased altogether with one final stab from my father that severed its last functioning data processor. It fell over devoid of power. My mother was in a lot of physical pain, along with the emotional turmoil of the programming she had been raised with. She yelled at the man to stay away from her. She'd never seen a man in her time. The belief that men were inherently evil and at blame for everything that had gone wrong, was still a very rampant ideology in those days.

"My father didn't listen to her though. When he drew close enough to her, she tried to stab him. He took her knife away. In the process of trying to help her, he knocked her out cold. The next thing my mother knew was waking up in a cavern. There was no natural light, but the man had lights everywhere.

"My father was very ingenious. There was water flowing in the cavern, and he used that to make electricity. Instead of awakening to the feeling of being abused though, it was to find that he had set her leg in place for her and even put it in a cast. He had tied her up though. That was good, because she tried to kill him again in order to be free. For a week he put up with that behavior from her without saying a word. He still faithfully tended to her needs, despite her best efforts to kill him.

"He fed her, gave her water, helped her to relieve herself and then nursed her through a fever that she developed. During the fever he no longer kept her tied up; she was too weak to even try to fight him. The fever lasted for three days. Once again, she would not have survived if it weren't for his efforts. She no longer fought him then.

"They begin to talk and tell each other about the other. My father was much older than my mother. He told her of what had happened in the time before, much as I am doing with you, right now. This is even his Bible. It's all I have left of him, along with the skills he gave me as a blacksmith.

"As time went by, my mother made a full recovery and could have left the caverns, but she chose not to. Despite the extreme age difference, the two of them fell in love. My mother had come to see that the propaganda she had been raised under was nothing but a lie, because she had a living example of a man that was no harm to any woman.

"They were together for about a year, when with surprise my mother found out she was pregnant with me. The Signal was still fully turned on in those days. Yet living underground, as he did, my father had avoided its effects on his reproductive abilities. Still, to them, my conception was a miracle. They tried to have more children in the years that followed, but it seemed that my father's seed no longer worked.

"He was so tender in his treatment of me. I will always remember him. My mother told me how it was in the world outside the caverns; and then when I was six she showed me. It was a shock to see. I had no wish to live in the world of women.

"Another year went by and somehow word of my father's survival was discovered. They came hunting us in the caverns. My father was well prepared for them. He took out many of the women with traps that my mother had helped him set up. The women retreated, as the cost to them became too great. That was when the Borgs were sent in.

"My father's defenses were able to take out several of them, but it was too much to take them all out. He got injured. My mother stood overtop of him, defending him as he lay dying beneath her. I watched from a hideout as both of them were burned to death. The remaining

Borgs did their best to destroy all evidence of my father ever existing, but they didn't find me.

"Along with this Bible and a few other things, I set out to leave the caverns, as they were no longer safe. I went from colony to colony as a girl. I lost my way spiritually for a while, but then I started my first blacksmith shop up when I was in my late twenties. The things my father taught me came back with a vengeance. As those lessons took hold once more, so did my father's faith, which he had shared with me and my mother. I will confess that for most of my life I have openly withdrawn from society and interacted with others as little as possible. In a way, I have for years blamed women, all women, for the death of my father and mother. That was not right of me and I apologize once more to all of you. I..."

A young brunette by the name of Ashandi, with a mouth known to be one noted for its sharpness and sarcasm in general, spoke up. "Let this be the end of your apologies to us. We do not want them, nor do we need them. You are sharing with us now of what you know, and that is enough."

For once no one disagreed with her. The change they were all feeling inside had apparently been working on this one's deeply rooted sarcastic self.

It was yet one more encouragement to all, not least of all to the brunette. She was short, but a formidable warrior in her own right.

Admittedly, her mouth was one of her weapons that she was most proficient with. Salantha had been surprised that she had stayed, as her mouth had earned her few friends and many enemies.

Feeling pricked in the spirit, Salantha made the choice that she would on the morrow try to befriend the girl. If the girl was really working to make a change in her ways, then Salantha wanted to take part in the process.

Even help her along, if she could. Such a thing would have been seen as weakness just a few days before, but right now, building community was strength itself.

One by one the women fell off to sleep, once more sleeping out in the open. The lions were still there, out in the dark just beyond the fire's light.

Like heroes in the dark they lounged about the women. Their senses picked up everything, which is why they heard the unmanned craft coming in the early hours of the dawn.

As dawn made its way forward in the sky, so did the male lion's warning followed by that of his cohorts. Startled, the women came awake and noticed the agitation of the lions. They took it for the warning that it was and hid themselves in burrows that they had dug into the ground, for just such a moment.

The cavitation noise of the flying craft grew louder as it self-controlled its path to buzz out over the colony. Its sensors picked up no life sign, other than the lions and other predatory animals that were nearby.

The message was clear to the algorithm as it computed the high likelihood that the compound was completely abandoned, else why would so many lions be meandering about. Decision made, the directive was issued that said, "*Colony abandoned. No further patrol necessary in this sector.*" With that notation edited into every local Borg's system, it moved off in its patrol elsewhere.

It went off in search of survivors, as a full inventory of women was currently being made to better aid the ongoing extermination efforts. With that occurrence, the women did not know immediately the full ramifications of what had just happened.

The lions had not only warned them, but by staying in place they had effectively made the case that the colony was abandoned. Therefore, it was now deleted from the enforcement map that the Borgs would utilize for planning out their genocidal operations.

In the mind of the algorithm there was no need to return, as new colonies did not come into existence in these days. Instead, they only became fewer and fewer.

One by one, they blinked out like candles in the dark. There was no worry or expectation of new colony construction, as there no longer existed the positive emotion within women to seek to build something new.

Those days were over.

CHAPTER EIGHT

The Encounter

Twelve Years Later

Ayayla

I eased forward as quietly as silence. The sounds of the forest were all about me.

Not one of the calls had an echo to it that would cause me to suspect it as being something else, but still..... I was not alone. I felt that reality very keenly.

What bothered me most was that I did not know what it was out there, somewhere, close by.

I had come to the forest with Shahaday.

I came every year to lay flowers on the grave of my parents. Salantha never let me come alone.

Usually it was her that came with me, but this time it had been Shahaday. Shahaday was a great warrior and someone I regarded closely as a friend; but one thing she wasn't adept at was being overly silent in her movements.

Not to say she was obsessively loud or clumsy, but she had a distinct set of sounds that she made with repetition when she moved, that I could have picked out if I had been blindfolded.

Some said my extraordinary hearing was a gift and truly it was, but right now it was letting me down. I heard nothing.

That is to say I heard everything about me, but not a thing in regard to what I felt was different. There was a distinct presence from somewhere close by, and I simply could not define what it was.

I felt threatened by it, but it was strange in that I did not feel within it the coldness of a Borg's calculation.

Three years ago, I had killed my first Borg. Last year, I had killed two more.

I knew what their presence felt like. What I was experiencing right now was not that.

Surely it could not be a creature either, as all predators had seemingly become our allies. What then could it be?

I paused next to a tree trunk. I peered around its curves, taking care to keep hidden from view as much as possible.

No visible threat moved in the understory vegetation.

Feeling overwhelmed by the sense of being watched, I moved forward, at the ready to pull my sword free and slay anything that moved. Whatever it was could clearly see me; of this I felt sure.

There was little point in hiding. As Shahaday had stayed with the horses, perhaps the smart thing would have been to retreat and make an escape from the forest if possible, but that was not my nature.

Today was a special day, the day I had come into being because of two people becoming one flesh. They were gone, but I would forever remember them, even as I loved them still.

I only got permission to come here once a year. I was not going away without having my moment of closeness with the past.

I slipped through the forest, scarcely breathing as my mind paid attention to every detail.

Every nuance of fluctuation, in hopes of spotting what was different. My senses came up empty again and again.

I was either imagining everything, or I was being invisibly stalked. I discounted the former as a possibility, and strongly disliked the notion of the latter.

Feeling threatened and highly on edge, I did not, however, feel that something evil was present. What then?

It hit me instantaneously. Eyes widening, I came to an abrupt stop.

Peering about, I let my mind crystallize into what I suddenly felt must be the truth. There was a man nearby somewhere.

Though cause for excitement, I was, however, more concerned about the feeling of aggression that I sensed. I didn't understand it or the watchful regard I felt myself being scrutinized under.

Gathering my breath, I called out with as even-toned of a voice as I could muster, "I mean you no harm. I have come to lay these flowers on my parents' grave. After I have done that, I will leave. Please do not attack. I mean you no harm." I spoke the words out into seemingly an empty scene of forest understory vegetation.

The sounds of the forest went on unabated, but I sensed a change. It was not the feeling of a Borg about to jump from concealment; rather it was the feeling of tension being released. I no longer felt as threatened.

Surely that was good, right?

I didn't know. Amalaka said that men thought differently than women, but there was little to go on as to explain how that related to this situation.

All I could say in the moment was that I no longer felt like my life was in jeopardy.

I could well imagine how a surviving male would have the objective of self-preservation foremost in mind, when he came across any unknown female. He might even be so objective as to simply slay any female he came across.

That is what women had been doing for years in regards to men. Why would it be any different from a male's perspective?

As I moved through the understory, I came to the sudden uneasy realization that if men thought the same way a woman did, then surely I would have already been dead. The unseen man was better than me at this game of remaining unseen.

I felt his presence as assuredly as ever, and yet I saw no one. Breathing heavy, I at last broke into the clearing that held as permanent testament to my existence the remains of my parents.

As usual, I lost all bearing. Virtually unconscious to all my surroundings, I stumbled forward as tears washed down my face.

No matter how many years passed by, it was always this way when I came to visit. The moment I saw the two crosses that bore the names of my parents, the memories came flooding back as if it were yesterday.

I remembered everything. I remembered the good days we'd had as a family. The smile and loving manner of my mother towards me. The tenderness and nurturing spirit of my father.

Their love for each other. Their love for me.

Sinking to my knees on the ground before the crosses, I laid the flowers down and kissed the ground. Crying harder, I lay stretched out on the ground as I hugged it.

It was the closest I would ever be again to either of them in this life, and it just wasn't enough.

Oh God, it wasn't enough!

The birds ceased their song in the overhead canopy of the forest, as the bitterly sad sound of weeping caused all creation witnessing the moment to cringe with commiseration.

The honesty of emotion being expressed was too heartbreaking for the sounding out of anything that could be interpreted as joy. Silent spectators, the birds watched, then with a furious flutter of wings, took off in flight in every direction.

Such a commotion normally would have alerted the figure sprawled out upon the ground to an unseen danger, but today it did not. The young woman at the grave site was at her most vulnerable.

The red lifeless eyes of a Borg burned into awareness. It had rested in stasis for almost a year in this spot, purely for the purpose of waiting for such a moment as this to occur.

This spot had been marked for extra oversight, given the appearance of a man here in the not-so-distant past. The grave had gone unnoticed for years, but last year it had been discovered.

The decision had been made to keep it under observation. Now the long wait was finally over. The progeny of the couple had returned.

A female, much too young, as the majority of humanity's last surviving females were all for the most part past prime childbearing age. Not this girl though.

She had to be destroyed.

The arm of the Borg lifted cautiously, as if fearing the creak of ungreased joints might give it away and give the girl a chance to escape. Arm now fully extended, it began to engage the cannon that would blow the girl apart at the seams and forever leave this forest uninhabited.

The red eyes flickered and the extended arm powerlessly fell back down with a clang to its side. In bewilderment at the failure to perform its directive, the Borg glanced down to the device that had burned a hole through its abdominal section plate.

Such a weapon as this was unknown. It had silently rendered the Borg paralyzed of any further movement.

It searched about with its remaining operational systems, but could detect no primary life-form save for the girl. Further alarm protocols rang out, as it became aware that the girl was now aware of its presence.

Instead of running off, however, the Borg took in the reality of her approach, coming directly at it. Machinery uselessly failing to respond, the Borg went through a meltdown as it tried to fulfill its mission directive.

Kill the girl, because she was a threat to the preservation of the System. It was the only surviving Borg left from the attack upon the girl's family so many years before.

Smoke arose from its circuitry as it tried to make new pathways in order to regain the function of its appendages. Then its moment of frenzy was over, as its head was sent careening from its paralyzed body.

The severed wires and circuitry sparked as it went rolling through the understory. At last it came to a stop, but the glowing eyes of an artificial intelligence had already ceased from letting off their glow.

Something that had never had life, now had no more impact on the elements that did possess life. The final artificial moments of its existence went unnoticed, though, as the girl it had sought to kill slowly reached out to touch the hole that had burned all the way through the Borg and severed its ability to properly function.

She'd chopped its head off, but the work of its destruction had been begun by someone else.

CHAPTER NINE

Feeling like a Fool

Wiping at my eyes and very much feeling like a fool, I let my gaze rise from the wound in the Borg's chest plate armor.

Slowly, I scanned the nearby forest.

I found myself gazing off to the right, not quite sure knowing why, as I said, “Thank you."

To my surprise I watched a branch shiver as something invisible made it to suddenly move. Eyes wide, I then did perhaps the second stupidest thing in my life besides losing awareness of my surroundings - I ran toward the spot that my unseen stalker had just been in.

I sheathed my sword. Surely another stupid mistake on my part.

Reaching the spot where I had seen the shiver of movement, I beheld the same movement of other branches out ahead of me. With my instincts and hearing doing double effort, I took off in pursuit.

I wasn't going to let this man escape. Not when he had just saved my life.

The burden to know more about him was overwhelming.

Why had he intervened?

What did such a thing mean?

Where had he come from?

Would I ever see him again?

Bursting free of the trees I splashed into a shallow creek. My eyes gazed searchingly at the opposing shore, but I saw no movement.

I cried out then as I felt a hand, a very large hand, which had a strength to it that caused me to quiver viscerally, even as physically it upended me into the strongest part of the stream's current. I fell flailing into the water and was washed several feet downstream.

Hacking out ingested water I came up to my feet, in many ways expecting an instant death, but there was no apparent threat present. No killing blow fell upon me.

Now more than ever I wanted to know this…man. Why did he not wish to be followed?

What was there about me that could possibly threaten him?

I shivered and it had nothing to do with the coldness of the water I stood halfway submerged in.

My gaze took in the opposing shore and landed on the spot where water was splashed against a rock that should be dry. I should have given up the chase, but I found myself drawn like a moth to the flame.

I pulled myself up onto the bank and took in the sight of a booted impression upon the damp soil. Setting my own foot into the impression that had been left, I had the thrill of a connection with someone else, such as I had never experienced before in my life, course through me.

I wanted more. So much more.

Tucking my wet hair back from my face, I followed the trail as it led into the forest. I came to a stony clearing and stopped abruptly as I felt his gaze once more upon me.

I could not describe it any other way. I simply felt him looking at me.

My gaze drifted off to the left. I saw nothing there that resembled the figure of a man.

I took a step closer in that direction anyway, as there was something that called out to me. Rocks literally blasted apart in front of me.

Crying out I stumbled back several feet. Breathing heavy I gazed about the area I had just started to approach.

Entirely uncertain about what to do, I waited. Then I daringly voiced my thoughts. "Why? I am no threat to you."

There was no answer, but still I felt him. Somehow it was clear he felt threatened by me just the same.

The reality of that made a thrill such as I had never known course through me. For the first time in my life I had the knowledge of what it felt like to be desired.

To be wanted like my father had openly hungered for my mother. This man wasn't running from me. He was running from himself.

Combing my long curly black hair back over an ear, as my heart came up with a plan, I remained boldly standing in the open. He could so kill me if he chose to.

It was equally obvious that he did not intend to do so. It was also obvious that he did not want me to follow him.

It was clear if there was to be anything between us, which I suddenly hungered for more than anything else, I would have to first earn this man's respect.

Speaking out I said, "I won't follow you anymore, but I..... I want more. You saved my life. I owe you. If you come back here to this exact spot in three weeks' time I will be waiting here with a gift for you. If you're too scared to come and accept it from me, I will understand and I will leave it here for you. I will not try to follow you or set a trap of any kind for you. I promise."

I turned away from where I felt him to be and started moving off. It was hard to do, as it felt like I was leaving part of myself behind.

At the edge of the sun dappled clearing I turned back and impulsively called out, "Please come."

That said, I turned away and started running.

~~~~~~~~~

I did not see the invisibility cloak electrically dissipate away from a tall form standing at the other edge of the clearing.

Nor did I see him come to stand where I had been standing.

Reaching down, his hand felt at the depression left by my foot, and his large form jerked much as mine had earlier.

Sighing he stood up to his full height. He moved off then in the opposite direction.

He seemed as reticent to leave as she had been.
~~~~~~~~~

CHAPTER TEN

In a Daze

Shahaday had scolded me unceasingly all the way back to the colony. While it was hard to hear, I knew it was lovingly meant.

I had acted rashly. I just hadn't been able to help myself though.

In some ways it had felt so right to follow after him. Now all I felt was an emptiness that was hard to define.

It was tempered by one thing. In three weeks I would see him, or at least I would feel his presence again.

Somehow that seemed to take precedence over everything else. In a daze of what that moment in the future would be like, I made it past the shocked and even angry outburst of the others as I headed for the blacksmith shop.

I knew they all loved me. Strangely, what they thought about me right now, though, didn't seem to matter as much as what he thought about me did.

Seemingly lost in a dream world, I passed by Amalaka who looked like she wanted to say something, but chose not to.

As if drawn by an unseen force, I gravitated to the forge that Amalaka had already been hard at work on. She had taught me everything she knew, and I had come up with a few things on my own in addition to that.

She said that I was even better at some things than she was, but I wasn't so sure about that.

Moving in what felt like a continued daze. I took out the makings of the finest ingredients for a sword, times two. I didn't even ask for permission. I just started the work.

The scraps of steel were leftovers from the Great War of the past when men had fought an all-out war to survive against the robotic forces of the Signal. These particular pieces had come off of something once called a 'Tank'.

Swords made of this material could cut through anything.

Hours went by. I sweated heavily as I made the pieces of steel to become one integrated solid core.

At last - I had achieved the start of what I intended to be my greatest creative endeavor.

The night was well advanced outside. Setting the billet of glowing steel off to the side I left the forge to cool down, as I stumbled my way over to lay down upon my bed.

Almost instantly I was dead to the world, but my thoughts remained on the silent man from the forest, who had saved my life.

~~~~~~~~~

Amalaka covered Ayayla up gently with a blanket. She had done nothing to stop the girl.

Her strange behavior was beyond worrisome. She'd told Shahaday remarkably little about what had happened other than that she'd had an encounter with a man, yet she had not seen him, and yet somehow he had saved her life.

In some ways that was enough.

Amalaka drew near to the piece of cooling steel. It was going to be a very large sword to be sure.

She had never attempted anything this big. This man must be big in order to wield something like this.

How did Ayayla know the dimensions to make it to if she had not seen him? She must be going on instinct or perhaps something else.

Had he touched her?

Amalaka glanced back to Ayayla contemplatively.

She glanced up as Salantha glided almost silently into the space. Salantha gave her a look in indication to Ayayla to which Amalaka shrugged.

She knew as much as she did about what was going on.

Salantha's gaze drifted down to the cooling rod of reforged steel.

“Do you think she expects him to come here to claim this blade when it is finished?"

Amalaka shook her head knowingly, “No, she will take it to him. It is her way."

Both women, who had each played the part of a mother, glanced toward the sleeping beauty sprawled across her bed.

Salantha spoke first, "Everything is about to change."

"Yes," Amalaka breathed out only to then whisper, “Thank God!"

Salantha nodded.
~~~~~~~~~

Glancing to Amalaka she said, "I must go and make ready, as I wish to be ready to greet this change. Will you help her make the sword?"

"Only if she lets me."

The two women shared a look at Ayayla, as the realization occurred to them both that the girl was no longer entirely their responsibility, as she seemed to already be looking elsewhere for accountability.

It was a bittersweet moment, but in their own way both women let go.

Salantha left. Amalaka turned to the now cooled steel rod. Stretching her hand out over it, she began to pray.

CHAPTER ELEVEN

Being Tested

Almost Three Weeks Later

I held the sword up and swung it. It wasn't easy to do with just one hand.

The blade would have been an unwieldy burden for me to have to wield in battle, but not for him.

My hand looked small as it gripped about the handle. It hadn't been made for my hand.

It had been made for his.

Thankfully, I'd had the memory of his grip about my ankle to use as a guide. In some ways it felt like his grip had never left me.

For the first time in what felt like an eon, my eyes opened up to awareness of my surroundings. My gaze left the blade to take in Amalaka and Salantha.

I blushed, and in return they both smiled.

"It is very nice, Ayayla. I think he will like it."

"He better!" Salantha intoned in response to Amalaka's statement.

Feeling even more embarrassed, I ducked my head down. Mumbling, I said, "I'm sorry I haven't been more present lately. I.....I really needed to get this done."

I looked up only to see both women nod understandingly.

"When are you taking it to him?" Amalaka queried softly.

"Tomorrow." Then my gaze tracking over to Salantha, I added, "Alone."

She held up her hands, and to my surprise she said, "I will not get in the way. I promise."

My surprise must have been evident for she added gently, "You are no longer a girl. You are a young woman and it is time for you to make your own way. I will always be here for you, though."

I set the sword down. Going over to her I enfolded first her and then Amalaka in a hug.

Whispering loud enough for both to hear I said, "Thank you for understanding."

Both women now hugged me. I may have lost my first family, but God had given me a second.

Now the question was, could I have even more?

Was that too much to ask for?

I hoped not, because I was asking for it with all of my heart.

~~~~~~~~~

The Next Day

Slowly, I moved into the stony clearing. Reaching the center of it I unburdened myself of the large blade. Setting it on a boulder, I unwrapped it of its covering.

It shone forth resplendently in the morning sunshine, as rays of light reflected brilliantly off of its polished expanse. It truly was my best work, ever.

Would he like it?

He clearly had a grasp of technology that most did not have. Would he think the gift of a sword as something childish next to his superior weapons?

His weapons were clearly far more superior, but..... this was what I was used to. This was my best effort to please.

I would take confidence in that. I drew back slightly and sat down to wait.

Would he come - or had all this been for nothing?

~~~~~~~~~

I waited all day. He did not come.

I should have left. However; I did not. Crying, I made it all the way through a sleepless night.

Sometime before dawn I must have passed out. A fly buzzing at my ear awoke me a few hours later.

Startled I got up to look about, but the clearing was empty. Turning back, I gasped.

The sword was gone!

The wrappings were folded up neatly where the blade had been. He'd come and gone.

Giving a bitter cry I looked about. Was this all there was going to be?

This acceptance of a gift with nothing further?

Sinking to my knees as despair reigned in my heart, I fought for some measure of control.

Thoughts ran through my mind. He couldn't be far.

I could track him down, but I'd said that I wouldn't. I had to be true to what I had promised, but.....

Crying, I sank my head to the ground.

I breathed out in a choked voice against the leafy litter, "I don't want to be alone, God. But if that is Your will for me, then please help me accept that."

Surging up to my feet I ran from the clearing, a place now enshrouded as one of intense bitterness for what had not happened.

I hadn't been simply offering a gift. I'd been offering myself, too.

He'd taken the sword though and left me to sleep. I had never felt more worthless in my whole life.

~~~~~~~~~

In the Clearing

The sound of horse hooves thundering in the distance echoed to the reality that she was gone. The electrically induced invisibility field faded away to reveal a man sitting on a boulder not five feet from where Ayayla had fallen into an exhausted slumber right before dawn.

He'd been there the whole time. From the very first moment she had entered the clearing.

He'd wanted to speak to her a thousand times, but.....

He'd had to be sure. Now he was.

There had been no ambush. No trap.

Just the honest attempt to please.

He glanced down to the blade that lay in his lap. It was a work of art.

It was her in a way, but holding the sword wasn't enough. He wanted more.

So much more.

Such desire was dangerous, but what was life if not for the risks one took.

He remembered her prayer and wondered with marvelment at how faith in the God he served had stayed in the hearts of some, while everywhere else the rest had seemed to turn their backs on the truth.

It wasn't just the scattered out colonies of women, but also the few men that were in existence as well.
~~~~~~~~~

There were other men out there. Some of them little better than savages.

He could easily have been like them, but he had chosen not to be.

He'd had a good example to inspire him to be otherwise. A very good example, indeed.

Still, it was hard to know who you could trust. Gazing down at the sword, he made the final determination that at last he had found a woman he thought he could trust.

He'd tested her and so far she'd gotten everything right. How far would she go in order to be with him, though?

Standing up, he headed out of the clearing in the direction that she had gone. Soon he would find out.

~~~~~~~~~

Amalaka rested back against a post of the smithy. Ayayla had returned hours ago - without the sword.

The girl had been inconsolable. At long last she had fallen asleep.

Amalaka didn't know what to think.

Closing her eyes she started to pray, only to hear an answer spoken audibly into her mind, **"He is coming."**

Amalaka's eyes opened.

Feeling shaken from within, she asked, "What do You want me to do?"

"He is going to test her. Let him."

Test her? What did that mean?

"Father, please I..... I don't want any harm to come to her, but.... I won't get in the way."

"I know you won't."

Amalaka went into the smithy and returned with a chair, which she sat down beside the door. Leaving the door wide open beside her, she sat down.

It was already evening; soon it would be night. Amalaka remained sitting as still as a statue, but with her eyes closed.

It was past midnight, when her arm lifted from her side to grasp strongly about the arm of something invisible that stood beside her in the doorway. All movement of the invisible entity stopped, as her hand remained in an unshakable clasp about his forearm.

It was a strong arm she held onto. She was the strongest woman she had ever encountered, but he was stronger than her by orders of magnitude.
~~~~~~~~~

It wasn't just the physical that made her feel dwarfed, but it was something more rooted in the spirit. This man had been tested in his life - severely so.

She let go of his arm and stood up. It was dark, but she saw his form materialize out of nothingness.

He was every bit as tall as her and very broad. Inclining her head forward she said, “She’s asleep. I will leave you now."

She turned away, but it was the man's hand that now gripped her arm implacably.

"You would leave your young charge in the hands of a stranger so casually?"

Amalaka looked back with tears in her eyes. “This is the hardest thing that has ever been asked of me by my God! Just the same, He told me not to get in the way, so I will not. It was wrong of me to lie in wait for you, but I hope it can be forgiven."

She made to shrug his hold off, but he released her instead. “There is nothing to be forgiven,” he assured. “Tell the one watching us over by the edge of the tall grass to be ready to leave in the morning. You are all no longer safe here."

He was gone then. With her eyes adjusted to the gloom of night she headed out to the edge of the compound. The closer she got, the easier she could make out the form of Salantha.

She stood there, still in the grass, even as an entire lion pride lay about her at rest. Her cheeks were wet with tears.

Before Amalaka could speak she choked out, "God said to let him pass. So I did."

Amalaka nodded. A long moment passed by and then she said, "He told me to tell you to get ready to leave in the morning. He said we are no longer safe here."

Salantha nodded.

Turning her gaze to Amalaka she asked, “What is he going to do to her?"

"I don't know." Amalaka confessed.

Both women sat down in the grass feeling more helpless than they ever had in life. They had learned something, though, in both of their now extended lives - you didn't get in the way of the Creator.

That didn't make it any easier for them to bear what felt like a betrayal of someone they both loved. Both women jolted as they heard Ayayla cry out, but they remained where they were.

Salantha whispered, "I don't understand."

Amalaka whispered in reply, "Neither do I, but.... we have to let this happen. It's not just about Ayayla. It's about all the others as well."

Salantha nodded.

She knew it was true, but it was like having a knife twisted in her gut to remain where she was and do nothing.

CHAPTER TWELVE

Reality Test

I breathed hard through my nose as I gazed up into the darkness with fear, even as the hand covering my mouth held my head immobile to the bed.

Both of my hands had risen to grasp at the hand over my face, but one was now secured down by a large knee, and the other lay pressed to the bed above my head, a prisoner to another's hand….. a hand that I remembered.

Abruptly, I went still. It was him.

"You're not going to bite me, are you?" came his voice out of the darkness. I reflected shock across all parameters of my being at the sound of its masculine appeal.

Numbly, I shook my head no. A movement only allowed because his force against my head had lessened considerably.

"You're not going to try to cry out again, are you?"

Numbly, I shook my head no.

I couldn't really see him, but it wasn't because he was cloaked invisibly, but rather because it was just so dark inside the blacksmith shop.

His hand left my mouth. I gasped in air.

My hands were released, only to rise in astonishment to press against him, as he now straddled down overtop of me fully. His knees were to either side of me, and while he didn't let all of his weight rest down onto me, he let a lot of it.

I'd never felt so helpless before. Breathing heavy, I lay there in the dark under him.

Both of my hands were once more the prisoners of his. He could do absolutely anything he wanted with me.

"This is what you wanted, isn't it?" came his deep voice out of the dark.

Wordlessly, I started to shake my head *'No'*, only to find myself nodding *'Yes'*, instead. I stopped the action in a blind panic.

What was wrong with me?

I looked past the dark form of him above me and outward into the room beyond.

"I did not hurt her or the one that the lions seem to be especially fond of."

I felt my breathing ease slightly, even though my hands remained a prisoner to his.

"Just the same, they are not going to come to your rescue; and if they did, I might have to hurt them."

"No, please! Don't do that!" I implored.

"So you can talk."

Shocked by everything that was taking place, I nodded.

I felt him chuckle as much as I heard it and - while I found a lot to like about it - I did not like this moment.

Why was my fantasy tormenting me like this in the night?

Why had he come here to torment me, when he could have done whatever he wanted with me in the forest?

Why take this risk?

Finding enough inner poise to speak, I at last managed to whisper, "Why did you come here?"

"To test you," came his steady response.

I blinked.

I made to speak, only his weight was shifting, even as I found my hands pressed out flat to the bed to either side of my head. I started to cry out, only to have it cut off by his lips on mine.

In startlement I lay still under the pressure of his lips and body. I couldn't get enough air suddenly. Gasping raggedly I turned my head to the side.

His lips kept kissing me though. My neck, my jaw, my ear.

"Please stop!" I begged out softly, not really expecting him to.

He did, though.

Speaking into my ear he said, "Not what you were expecting, is it?"

Wordlessly, I nodded.

One of his hands left mine. My hand still lay pressed back to the bed though, as if he still held it fast there.

In that moment I realized that some part of me wanted this, while the rest of me was horrified by it. His hand grasped my jaw and turned my head back to face him.

"I will leave if you ask me to. If I do, however, it is the last time you will ever see me."

My hand that had been freed, involuntarily clutched at his shoulder all of a sudden. I had never felt so much muscle.

My body feeling as if it had been dipped in flames had my hand fleeing back away from his shoulder. He chuckled again. When he did I felt a curious ache open up in me that yearned to hear it happen again.

What was wrong with me?!

"You don't know what you want, do you? I should leave."

My other hand was released, even as his heavy form started to pull back from mine altogether. Both of my hands seized about his forearms.

He stopped moving. I didn't let go.

I felt my body start to shake; maybe I had been shaking the whole time. My hands were disgustingly sweaty, but I still didn't let go.

The idea of him leaving for forever was more than I could bear the thought of. I did nothing to stop the descent of his head towards mine once more.

I didn't close my mouth as his lips fell down once more upon mine. In fact, I opened my mouth up further for him.

With an inexperienced jolt, I registered him take full advantage of my surrender. His mouth literally consumed me and I did nothing to turn away from its domination.

Air passed over my swollen lips and dimly I realized that he was no longer kissing me. I didn't know what was happening or how far this was going, but what I did know as desperately real in the moment, was that I didn't want him to leave.

To that end I was prepared to even suffer, for I very clearly felt how much he wanted me. And yet of all the things to come to mind in this moment, I found my lips asking, "Why did you let me go in the forest, if you want me so much?"

"I had to know."

"Know what?"

"Whether you were a person of your word or not. It would have been easy to take what I wanted, but maybe that was what you wanted, too. Maybe you wanted to be without choice. Tonight, I've given you a choice. You can ask me to leave and I will. If I stay, you know what might happen. We're no longer in a forest and I am no longer a mythical creature of a girl's idle fantasy. I'm here. I could break you in half. I could give you pleasure, and yet I can certainly cause you pain. All of these are realities of any relationship between a man and his woman. Right here in this moment there is no fantasy, no childish imagination at play. I have every ability to use you for my own pleasure, and yet you haven't asked me to leave. Why is that?"

Swallowing, I struggled with words for a moment before I managed to breathe out, "I don't want to be alone."

"Then get a pet."

His statement was so unreal to the moment that I gave a spurt of laughter. How could I possibly laugh at a time like this?

Maybe it was because I knew I could trust him.

Quickly sobering I responded, "I want to be your woman."

"You do?"

I nodded.

"Because you don't want to be alone?"

"No, that was a bad answer. I....I.... it's more than that."

"Well, we have all night, so tell me what it is you really want."

Gazing up into his darkened face I whispered, "I want what my mother had."

He was quiet for a moment and then stated, "You knew your father."

"Yes."

"He threatened your mother with abuse."

"No!!!"

"Then what is it of him you seem to think you see in me?"

"I....I... I don't actually think..... think you'd do what you're threatening me with."

"You don't think I'll leave and never come back?"

My hands left his arms to grasp at his shoulders as with desperation I said, "No, I believe that! I.... it's the other stuff."

"The other stuff?"

"Yes," I replied in a small voice.

He shifted against me in a way that left no doubt as to his desire, and my face flamed in the dark.

Passionately he asked, "Are you really so naive as to believe I wouldn't cause you pain?"

I didn't let go of his shoulders. He was not leaving, no matter what it took to convince him.

An idea came suddenly to mind. I pulled up with my hands and briefly kissed him.

My lips fell away from his as I lay back on the bed beneath him. I didn't know what would happen.

Finding words, I managed to get them out, even as I felt the intensity that vibrated through him like a storm that had suddenly spun out of any control, to bring it back to a state of calmness.

"It's not that I doubt that you can cause me pain. While it's true I don't want to be alone, that has little to do with how I've felt ever since I've come in contact with you. Yes, I am scared of you. Yes, maybe I didn't know what this was all about - man and woman..... that is until now. I...... being like this with you right now..... it is very overwhelming. I didn't know it could be so terrifying to be under the authority of a male. I still don't want you to leave, though. I want you to stay. I want..... no..... I need to be yours. I can't explain it well, but I'll try.

"Ever since I felt your eyes on me, I've felt claimed by you somehow. I willingly surrendered everything that I am to you, even though at the time I really didn't know what I was doing. Maybe that was stupid of me, but.... I..... you're not my father any more than I'm my mother. I don't know if I could ever have what they had..... with you..... but something says I could..... and I...... I'm willing to risk everything to find out if it's true or not."

I finished the last words with all my breath gone, and very little faith remaining that I had said enough to convince him to stay.

For a moment nothing happened and my terror grew. He was going to leave.

At last I heard him sigh.

I gripped onto his shoulders harder as I feared the worst, that my declaration hadn't been enough of an answer for him. Oh God, what could I say to make him stay?!

We were both moving then, as he shifted the two of us. I went willingly along with the urging of his hands, not really sure what was happening.

Eyes wide in the dark I registered the sensation of what it felt like to be cuddled up against his side with his arm about me. I could feel the heavy beat of his heart that my ear lay against.

He could probably feel mine, too, as it felt like it was about to thud its way out of my chest. His hand came to clasp possessively over my hip and then, strangely, that was it.

He just lay there in the dark taking up most of the bed, as I half laid on top of him, not moving.

Whispering, I ventured out with exploratively, "You're not going to....." My words trailed away.

His voice sounding tired he said, "I only came to test you. I'm not a monster or an animal that takes whatever it wants."

Slowly, I let my hand splay out over his belly. A moment later I let my thigh slide over the top of his leg, more than it already was.

I found this position very comfortable. Everything was an entirely new experience, beyond what I could have ever imagined.

As I lay there in the dark with all my senses awash with the reality of him, I felt an up-swell of emotion take hold of me. He was most definitely not a monster.

In fact, he seemed more like my father with each passing second.

"What's your name?" I asked softly.

"Tagan," he intoned, even as I felt the rumble of his words before they even left his lips.

I repeated his name aloud before shyly saying, "My name is Ayayla."

"Beautiful name for a beautiful woman. It suits you," he said. I could feel on an even deeper level than the auditory that he really meant what he had just said.

The feeling of being complimented by a man was breathtakingly new.

Somehow I felt special, because he thought my name was beautiful. Because he thought I was beautiful.

Time passed by. I had almost thought him to be asleep when he said, "Your sword that you made for me….. never have I seen a finer blade. Your workmanship was flawless. You are truly gifted and I'm honored that you went to the task of making something that fine for me."

Feeling very overwhelmed by his words, along with the emotion I heard in them, I found myself suddenly blinking back tears.

"I had a very good teacher," was all I was able to manage to get out, but bodily I snuggled all the more earnestly into him as I suddenly craved being close to him.

I wanted more.

More compliments.

More conversation.

More of his touch on me.

I could go on, but I forced myself to refrain. I didn't know much about intimacy obviously, but I could guess it was a strain to be both as desirous as he had been only a short time ago, only to now suddenly cut off all passion as he had.

Again, the reality was made clear that he was not a monster. In fact, he seemed to be incredibly in control of himself, which made him more characteristically similar to my father by the moment.

Sleepily I asked, "How do you know the language of the women of these lands?"

The hand on my hip tightened abruptly. What had I said wrong?

I didn't think he was going to answer me, when suddenly he did. "When I was a boy, I was captured by a colony of women."

My head lifted off his chest, even as I came up on my elbow to look at him in the dark.

"They didn't sell you off to the Borgs to be disposed of?"

"No. They had other uses for me in mind. They used me, until I managed to escape at sixteen with another man that they held prisoner."

His hand still lay in a tight grip over my hip. I could only imagine what his early life must have been like under those conditions.

How he must hate women!

Several tears slid down my cheek as the reality took hold of what his past had been like, what mine had almost been like. His grip on my hip lessened.

His free hand came up and gently pressed my head back down to his chest. I let him do so, without a fight.

As my cheek rested against him once, more I felt his fingers come to wipe away the moisture on my other cheek. The gesture from a hand that was so powerful seemed beyond incredibly tender in the moment.

Haltingly I said, "The women here - they're no longer like that."

"I know. Or I would have killed every last one of them."

His fingers were still stroking softly about my face in a manner that said he found delight in what he touched.

For perhaps the first time, I realized truly how much he must be restraining himself. It was humbling and it made me want to give him everything of myself even more so, but clearly he had decided that tonight was not the night.

Feeling burdened to share more of myself I whispered, "That almost happened to me….. I mean….. what happened to you as a boy."

"I'm glad you were spared that," was all he said by way of reply.

Thinking about the emotions he must have towards women I asked, "What made you not kill me outright when you first saw me?"

"You have no idea how beautiful you are, do you. Of course you don't; but that wasn't everything. The way you, at risk to yourself, continued on to lay flowers down at your parent's graves did almost everything in terms of convincing me that you were different."

He didn't say anything more after that. He'd already said so much.

"I….. I've never been with…… with anyone. I….. if you want you could….."

"Go to sleep, Ayayla. I will take you to be my wife, but not tonight."

Still worried, I breathed out, even as his fingers now played in my hair. "You won't leave?"

"I won't leave without you."

I closed my eyes trustingly. This man could have my everything.

Somehow I already felt loved by him. When had that happened?

From the moment of thinking I was about to be killed in my sleep, to the here and now, I was not sure, but just the same, it had.

CHAPTER THIRTEEN

"I will."

Dawn was just beginning to light up the interior of the smithy when two anxiously nerve-wracked women peered inside around the still open door. The sight they saw was not what they had expected to see.

Pulling back from the door, they both met each other's gazes as a palpable sense of relief shot through them, having just seen the contented form of their daughter still fully clothed and deeply ensconced in the arms of an equally clothed male.

Their incessant worrying had been for naught. Quietly they stole away from the smithy, as it just felt wrong to disturb the sleeping couple any sooner than they had to.

Feeling they were a safe distance away, the women stopped.

Salantha winked at Amalaka and said, "I guess she passed the test."

Before Amalaka could respond, they were addressed jointly by Ashandi. "We've got everything packed."

Her gaze, leaving them behind, centered in on the smithy. She quickly added all on one long breath, "Is he really in there with her? What does he look like? Are there more where he came from?"

Amalaka sighed, "All will be known in time. For now, you leave them alone! If you so much as….."

Sytana standing nearby abruptly gasped, only to exclaim, "Oh God, I hope there's more like him!"

Amalaka turned to see that the man had indeed arisen. Salantha had already headed out toward him.

Amalaka's gaze drifted from her to the usually sharp-witted Ashandi, who usually always had something to say.

In the moment; however, the woman appeared to be speechless. Amused, Amalaka's gaze left Ashandi to meet Sytana's shocked gaze.

Stumbling with her words Sytana said, "Men….. they're very…… different looking."

"Very." Amalaka affirmed.

Despite the tension filled night she was now feeling very good about everything taking place, especially as she took in the sight of Ayayla shyly standing beside the man, as he conversed with Salantha. Though clearly embarrassed the girl didn't look like she wanted to be anywhere else than where she was standing beside this man's side.

What had started out as an uncertain morning had blossomed into a radiant one full of promise. Feeling overjoyed she slapped Ashandi on the back hard.

The woman jerked as she was brought back into focus. Amalaka had been about to say something else, but she held it back as she suddenly caught sight of something seemingly fragile in the woman's gaze.

Ashandi perhaps more than any other had changed the most in terms of their old lifestyle. It was a surprise to Amalaka continually that she had been one of the ones to stay.

She had been in a very committed relationship with one of the women who had left.

Gently, Amalaka said, "Men are very different, but that said, I don't think you're going to regret your decision to stay here all these long years for the coming of this day to finally be realized."

Sytana, missing all the subliminal subtext going on between the two broke in to say anxiously, "But there's only one of him!"

"Now, don't be worried about that. God will provide." Amalaka affirmed reassuringly.

To that Sytana nodded affirmatively, as she squared her shoulders and said, "Why yes, He will."

She headed off then leaving Ashandi alone with Amalaka.

Glancing to Amalaka the other woman haltingly spoke, "What if….. what if…… I can't…… with a man?"

Amalaka took the brunette's head in her hands and gazing into her eyes she said with force, "You will."

"I…."

"Just shut up for once, Ashandi and believe what someone else has to say. Can you do that for me?"

Slowly, Ashandi nodded, and then softly Amalaka heard her say, "I will."

CHAPTER FOURTEEN

Jealousy & Prophecy

Ayayla

We were really leaving. It wasn't a dream either.

I'd walked right into a post at the smithy earlier. The one whole side of my face still hurt.

This was real.

I'd been staring at him and.... well, I'd forgotten about the post.

Was this...... infatuation, normal?

I..... he was just so good to look at..... I didn't even have anything to judge by, except my father, but well...... that was kind of weird to think about. He was not my father.

He was....... mine?

I glanced about, only to see that I wasn't the only one gazing at the man, who had just assumed leadership of the group virtually uncontested. Salantha hadn't resisted and he had in no way disrespected her either, as he had gently assumed control.

In fact, he had her right up there by his side right now at the head of the column of riders. She didn't look at him as a lot of the others did and that made me feel a lot better.

I didn't like the reality behind the other's gazes though, that said, I couldn't fault them for it.

Amalaka was riding by my side and her face wore a knowing look upon it. She knew.

She confirmed it then by saying, "I believe the word for it is jealousy."

My face heated, but honestly I admitted, "I don't want to share him."

A moment passed by before I added, "But I will if I have to."

Amalaka looked hesitant to speak, but knowing that I needed to hear what she had to say I said, "What is it?"

"That decision isn't yours to make. It's his. It's not that you don't have rights, but you don't control what he does. Your job is to support him. Help him in any way that he needs. You don't get to make decisions for him though. Do you understand that, Ayayla?"

I nodded, as her words hit me hard.

"I'm scared," I admitted.

Amalaka surprised me by saying, "I think that is a good thing."

I looked at her askance, my surprise quite evident.

She clarified her statement then for me, as one with extreme patience for someone slow to understand something that they didn't want to hear in the first place, "I don't know exactly how it was before, but what I do know of the past, even before my time was that men no longer had the respect of women. Everybody did whatever they wanted to. There was no accountability.

"There were rules put in place that made it so that mated pairings essentially failed and as a result men stopped marrying women and then a lot of them even stopped mating women altogether. There was plenty of blame everywhere to be sure, but I think when men were outlawed from being themselves, being masculine that is, well it was maybe the end of something very important.

"When they couldn't be themselves they abandoned women, who in turn tried to act like men. For some reason they were allowed to do that, while men were told to be more like women. It all went really wrong, Ayayla. I think everyone lost sight of the way of creation.

"Man was made first and then a woman was made in order to serve the man's needs. Not hers. But the man was told to love the woman, more than his own self. When a man is kept from being himself, how then can he love a woman? How can a woman respect a man, if he is not his masculine self? There is an order that needs to be followed if there is to be any hope at harmony in a relationship between a man and a woman.

"While we are all precious in the Creator's eyes it also goes that in this physical life men and women are not equal, and nor do I think that they should seek to be so. We were created different. Both men and women were created with a purpose and that purpose was not for us to drop all of our differences and seek to be the same as each other. Rather in our differences we each supply what the other needs or lacks. And because of this there will always be a disparity of power in a healthy relationship, if there is no disparity then there was no headship and if there is no headship then there can be no authentic relationship.

"Ayayla, I speak all that I do with no real life experience of my own, but I am old and I have pondered on these things for a very long time. If you would hear any wisdom from me then it would be this. Focus all your heart on meeting his needs first. Give unselfishly of yourself to him. Indeed, I ask you to pour your life out before him and hold nothing of yourself back. You might well lose everything, but putting myself in the position of thinking like a man, I think that is what he wants most from you.

"No matter how you try you cannot make him love you. Nor should you be jealous of what he does. You just focus everything you are into meeting his needs, obeying what he says and helping him however you can. I think if you do this, if you let him rule over you, you will have everything you could possibly ever want in return.

"Loving someone always comes at a great risk, Ayayla. You know this. Serving someone unconditionally can mean the sacrifice of everything you hold dear, but it's how I think he was made to experience love. I think every man was made to feel love from a woman willing to give of herself to the very last fiber of her being in service to him. Do your part of this unequal equation that was set in place at the beginning of creation. If you do, I think it will provoke him to do his part of the equation, which if he does will make up for everything you've given up for him.

"It is a risk though, as he might take all that you give him and return nothing. Just the same, I hope that you take this risk, because if he does do what he was ordered to do by his God, then you will experience all that God wanted you to enjoy in this life as a woman."

Nodding emotionally, I said, "I will. Thank you, mother."

Amalaka, looking embarrassed, glanced away.

I reached out and touched her arm. She glanced back to me and I saw a tear in her own eye.

Emotionally she said, "I really want this to work out between you too! Everything went so wrong in the past and…… I want there to be a better future! I….."

"There will be. I will do everything you have advised me to do and one day I will tell my daughters just the same as you have done today for me."

Now openly crying, Amalaka nodded, and said, "You better!" Her voice was soft, but entirely serious in message.

I nodded, it was a promise.

I felt a tug on my other arm and glanced over to Shahaday.

Giving me a tender look she said, "Don't be jealous of us, Ayayla. We all know that he's yours and I feel convinced that he will remain only yours, but like Amalaka said, that's his choice. But, I think I speak for all of us, when I say he only seems to have eyes for you."

My face heated and then forcing myself to I glanced back. All the others were smiling at me.

Sytana teased, "I'm only looking because, well….. how can I not? I don't mean anything by it, Ayayla. Looking at him helps me dream about…… well, you know. I…… you're very blessed, Ayayla. We are your friends. We want your relationship with him to succeed as much as Amalaka does. Seeing you interact with him, well - it's teaching us all and yet you are the youngest of all of us by many years.

"We all want what you have. And yet we all haven't aged even a single day in over twelve years. We know the Creator is at work. We know we've been reserved by Him for a better future. Each of us is not perfect, but each of us is going to try to do our very best when we are blessed with mates of our own.

"I can say, for at least myself, that your man is not my master. I can almost see my master at times, but he's still a blur to me. Since we've been riding today I feel like I'm finally headed out toward him and the future we will have together with one another."

Several others murmured and the consensus was that many had the same feeling. A moment of silence formed and I sat upon my horse completely humbled.

The stillness was broken by a despondent declaration. It was Ashandi, "I can't feel anyone."

Surrounding riders looked at her with concern and I realized all over again how much all of these women were my family. I would do anything to wipe away the forlorn look in Ashandi's eyes.

Outwardly I forgot how I had been humbled, even as inwardly I begged, 'Please God, help her!'

My lips opened and my voice came out loudly, being a shock to my own ears, "Ashandi?"

She glanced at me. Meeting her gaze I said with stated finality, even as I felt it in the words as I spoke them, as if it was something already done, "He has a scar much like Salantha does, only it's just one scar, but it goes down his face over his eye like one of hers does. When the time is right he will pull you up to safety, but until then you must climb. You must!"

Ashandi's face wore a look of shock at my words. Equally shocked I glanced from her to Amalaka and whispered out, "I don't know why I said all of that!"

Amalaka, far from looking shocked as a lot of the others did, was instead smiling, "It is called prophecy. Long have I wished to see it in action. God has spoken through you, because you invited Him to use you as a messenger for His will to be known to someone that He loves. Do not be afraid. It is a very good thing." glancing back she stated with emphasis her words directed at a very stunned looking Ashandi, "it will happen if….." she paused thematically before adding with import….. "if you do what has been asked of you."

Shakily, Ashandi nodded.

After a long moment Sytana pulled in alongside her. Giving Ashandi a mischievous look she said, "Your man sounds dangerous. I wonder how he came by the scar. Probably in a fight."

"Maybe with a bear." one of the others suggested.

"Ohhh that could be it. No doubt he killed it too." Sytana rejoined.

"Oh stop it." Ashandi murmured, looking embarrassed as others suggested even more methods of derring-do.

Embarrassed or not though there was a slight smile playing at the corner of her mouth.

I looked forward. It was really going to happen - what had been spoken through me to her.

It was awe inspiring to know I had been used to speak hope into the life of another. It made me feel even more humbled.

It also terrified me. The reality that God would use me to effect change on Earth was almost limitless, seemingly in the ways that I might mess it up and get His message not delivered or messed up in some other way.

I glanced at Amalaka. She seemed to be reading my thoughts as usual so I just out-and-out said it, "I'm scared in a whole different kind of way now."

"I think that too is a good thing." She said knowingly.

She was probably right. My gaze left her to take in Tagan.

I could look at him for hours. He and Salantha were riding ahead of us by a sizable lead.

Hopefully he hadn't heard any of this. At that moment he turned and looked at me and I knew.

He'd heard everything!

To make matters worse he smiled slightly and of all things winked at me. I might have fallen off my horse then if it hadn't been for Amalaka's steadying hand.

"Steady now, darling. You don't need any more injuries today."

Truly, I did not, but if there had been a hole close by I would have gladly crawled into it. His hand moved in a gesture.

He wanted me to come up there with him.

Oh God have mercy!

Obediently, I urged my horse forward, even as I felt like dragging back on the reins with reluctance. What was he going to say?

Oh this was going to be bad…… and humiliating!

I drew up beside him with my face feeling like it was in flames.

I couldn't look at him. I wanted to though.

With a gasp I felt myself jerked out of the saddle. Before I knew it I was riding astride his horse seated behind him.

I had to hold on to him in order not to fall off. Through the abrupt transition of my bodily form to his horse he hadn't said anything.

Why had he done this? The thought came to mind then - he hadn't asked anyone else to do this.

Any of the others would have all heartily agreed to such a seating arrangement, but I was the one that was near him. I was the one that got to touch him.

He'd made a statement without even speaking a word. In a way he'd given me value that I'd never had before in the eyes of others.

My fingers curled into the leather of his vest. He smelled so good.

He felt good too.

Hurriedly, I glanced to the side to see if Salantha could see how besotted I was with this man, but she wasn't there. Where was she?

I glanced back, she was riding beside Amalaka with the reins of my horse in one hand. Beyond her both Ashandi and Sytana made the suggestive hand signals of holding onto an imaginary someone and openly kissing that someone.

Their actions were quickly picked up by the others. I turned my head forward and pressed it against his back in an effort to hide.

I was never living this moment down.

His voice came out then soft enough so that only I could hear it, “They really love you.”

It wasn't a question, but rather it was a definitive statement.

Yes, they most definitely did love me. I knew that, but I was still embarrassed.

His next words took all my embarrassment away though, “I will love you too. I promise.”

My arms came around him more. He was really big and….. powerful.

I liked it. I liked it a lot.

Then so softly that I doubted he could tell that I'd done it, I kissed the back of his vest. It wasn't enough though.

I wanted him to know. Stretching up I wetly kissed the back of his muscle corded neck.

His body seemed to vibrate with an intensity that was thrilling to feel at the connection of my lips with his skin.

He said nothing though, but in the background I heard Shahaday say, “Ohhh! She really did it!”

Yes, I'd done it. They could talk about it all they wanted.

I rested the bruised side of my face against his vest. It seemed to make it feel better.

I closed my eyes. I was very happy to be where I was.

So happy, I even silently let God know all about it in the spirit, even as with my earthly conscience I focused on holding onto something very good.

~~~~~~~~~

Amalaka and Salantha

Amalaka in an aside to Salantha said, "I hope she doesn't fall off the horse. I have never seen her so clumsy before."

With a smirk Salantha said, "He wouldn't let her. The man has the reflexes of a cat."

Amalaka had noticed much the same.

Glancing to Salantha she asked, "I saw you two talking earlier. Mind sharing?"

Salantha grinned big, "He wanted to know about her."

"Oh really?"

"Yes, really. I mean everything too. Her favorite color, flower, time of day, yada yada yada. The man's thorough let me tell you."

"So you told him these things?"

"Oh yes! I told him everything and I mean everything."

"Good, I'm sure he will put it to good use."

Salantha nodded. Soberly then, she added, "He told me some other things too. I'll tell you later."

Amalaka nodded, understanding that it was something she didn't want the others to know just yet.

"How are you taking it with him assuming control of everything?"

"It was time. No..... actually, it's a relief." Salantha admitted.

"You're a very special woman, Salantha. Not many could let go of power as easily as you have."

Salantha gave Amalaka a look before stating, "You're rather special yourself, dear."

Glancing around the group at large she stated reflectively, "So are all of us."

Amalaka nodded. It was true.

They were all very blessed, but all Amalaka could take in at the moment was the contentment of seeing the way Ayayla seemed to have melted into the stalwart form of their new leader. The poor man was no
~~~~~~~~~

doubt driving himself crazy with having her pressed up against him like that, but he'd made a definitive statement by his actions.

Ayayla was his.

He had all the attributes of a great leader but his tenderness with Ayayla in the moment was what had brought her to love the man. Not only him though - seeing the way the two of them were with each other - made her love God, the creator of all she was witnessing take place, even more.

Amalaka blessed her God with praises that fell like whispered adorations from off her lips. Salantha was doing the same.

CHAPTER FIFTEEN

A Long Brutal War

Ayayla

That night we camped at what I thought was the entrance of a cave, but with a little discovery found out it was what Tagan called a train tunnel. He said that the other end of it was now buried in rubble and that it was no longer passable.

Once it had been used by men for shelter from the Signal, but by the time the Borgs had found them they had become little better than cannibals.

As the fire burned before us all we listened to a man's elegant speech of conversation. In large part it was an entirely new experience for everyone.

What made it all even more amazing was that I got to sit right next to him.

Everything about him was mesmerizing for me. He was a good bit older than me, but that wasn't an issue other than it was my fervent wish that he lived to be as old as I ever got to be.

He had yet to physically claim me, but I felt his claim over my life just the same. It was like I was no longer my own.

It was different. It was a little scary. It was entirely exhilarating.

As much as the man was the focus of my every thought so now was the voice that spoke with intelligence as he answered questions being directed at him from all those present. In a way it seemed like he knew everything and yet I had never encountered someone so humble.

It was disarming, even as with sincerity I believed everything he said, as if it was the Gospel truth. My eyes rose to his face as he answered Shahaday's question of why the colony had suddenly become in danger.

"The Borg waiting by the gravesite in stealth mode likely had a mission protocol to wait in hiding just past a year's time, as any likely visit to the site would be done on a yearly basis. They may not be human, but they know our patterns. They find that Borg decommissioned they'll turn the place upside down, especially because they have a mission log of a man once existing there."

A moment passed by. Idly Salantha said, "I've never been this way so far before. Always, at least in my younger days, we drifted around the open plain areas or the borders of the forest. We were told by the women before us to avoid the mountains and the deep forest as that was where the Borgs congregated the most."

"It's also where most of the men fled to. A lot of them went underground. Many of them became something worse than…" he paused for a moment before completing his statement, "…the women of the plain country."

A lot of the women ducked their heads down, even as tears started dripping off of their faces.

"Hey!" Tagan interjected into the sudden somberness of inner contrition that was taking place. All of the women looked up.

Earnestly gazing at seemingly all of them at once he said, "I'm no saint either. I've done things, hard things - things I'm ashamed of just to survive. This life we live now isn't about survival anymore. I don't sacrifice anymore of my soul to just draw breath for one more day. Right now is about being human. All of you are survivors, but like me you've all accepted a higher calling for your life than simply seeking out whatever your base desires may be. We don't exist solely for ourselves anymore. We exist to fulfill a purpose."

He pointed upward and we all knew what he meant even as he added, "His purpose. Maybe we can't forget what we've done or what we've been a part of, but He has. We are saved by Grace through belief in His Son, who lived the perfect life that none of us have come close to or would ever be able to achieve on our own. You're forgiven, so do your best to move on and embrace the future He has for all of you."

Heads everywhere nodded, even as tears were wiped away, only to be replaced with fresh ones and yet the mood of the place was no longer one of somber self-reflection, but rather one tinged by the joy of renewal that they had all experienced in their lives.

Sytana spoke haltingly, "Are there others like you out there?"

Tagan looked at her directly and said, "No."

She blinked. He could have left it at that, but he elaborated for her, "Men are different from one another, even as some of you women are very different from one another and I am not talking about outward appearances. Sytana, there are just as many evil-minded men, as there are evil minded women in existence. We here are a minority in terms of what's left of humanity in terms of our inner belief structure. Am I saying there's no hope for you to find a mate of your own? No, I am not, but I don't want you to fantasize about the men that are left as if they are something more special than you. You are very special and it just might be you that takes the lead in helping a man become more like you in the spirit that you are in possession of through the Most High."

Sytana blinked again. Haltingly she replied, "I….. I thought men were supposed to lead us."

"In the physical realm, yes, but in the Spirit - there have been many women throughout history who led their men to salvation. As loyal as you should be to your mate, your first responsibility as a souled individual is to be obedient to your God and not the will of a man should it go against what God has told you to be or for what He has said to do. You have a responsibility for yourself spiritually that you must maintain. This means even turning your back on something you want in the physical, if it's not what God wants for you. It is not an easy thing."

"Is that why you didn't show yourself to me when I brought you the sword?" I asked unconsciously.

Immediately my face heated, but no one was laughing, this was a serious moment.

"Yes, I had to know you were right for me beyond simply being attracted to you. I as a man have a responsibility to put God ahead of everything else, even a wife and children. He is my headship that I must obey even at the cost of everything. That said, it was God who told me to make the journey to come find you. I didn't believe Him at first, as I have grown to not trust the desires of my flesh ever, but I obeyed Him. Then I wanted what I saw, but I waited, until I was told that I could have you. I have learned that there is nothing worth having in life if it doesn't match the Father's plan for my life."

His eyes were on me and softly I nodded. Really, I was overwhelmed.

I really wished that no one else was here right now, because I wanted to kiss him. I…. I wanted to be one flesh with this man so badly.

It had to be obvious to everyone what it was that I wanted. Embarrassed I started to get up to flee away, but his hand on my shoulder brought me back down.

He wasn't looking at me though, even as he tucked me in against his side companionably. I couldn't bring my gaze to look up.

Salantha's voice spoke, "You have nothing to be embarrassed about, Ayayla."

"No, you do not." Tagan affirmed.

Then he said, "I can assure you; however, that I'm not going to give everyone here a tutorial in the art of lovemaking just to assuage the plea I see in your eyes to be one with me."

I hid my face in against him, even as several, if not all of the women gave a spurt of laughter. I was so embarrassed and yet I sensed I had never been so respected by someone before.

He'd let everyone know again the depths of his commitment to me. I hadn't even done anything it seemed to deserve it and yet he just kept giving it to me.

Was this love? It had to be, because he hadn't gotten anything in return that I could see.

Ashandi spoke and inwardly I thanked her for diverting the conversation from me, "Where are we going?"

"I found a place, well actually, I was led to a place years ago in the mountains. It has some...... special features to it that kind of make it a fortress, only one without walls. It's hard to describe exactly, as it involves technology that you have been without the use of for several generations. Really the only thing it lacks are the right kind of women. You might say that problem has been solved with the advent of all of you."

Shahaday stated what was on the minds of many instantly upon the heels of that last statement, "There's other men.... there in this special place that you're taking us to?"

Tagan's eyes seemed to twinkle as he replied, "A few."

Shahaday's eyes pleaded for a more accurate answer.

Tagan added, "There's twenty three to be exact."

The jaws of most of the women seemed to hit the floor at that statement.

"Twenty three men?!" Shahaday whispered out loud almost in disbelief, but we all knew that Tagan just wasn't the kind of man to lie about anything.

What made that odd was that we for the most part had no other man to judge that off of, but when it came to him you just knew he had to be a man among men.

Again, I felt a tremor pass through me. I was so unworthy of what I had been given.

My gaze flickered up and met Amalaka's across the fire. She shook her head 'No'.

Letting my breath out I straightened up slightly. Unworthy or not I was going to give this man my best, even if I had to die trying.

I really, really didn't want to die though. But..... I glanced at him..... I would gladly die for him.

Shahaday seeming very dazed said, " Twenty three and not counting Ayayla that leaves thirty of us."

"Oh don't count me." Amalaka quickly interjected.

Salantha spoke up, "And why not?"

"Well, I.... I'm over ninety years old. It's...."

"No, it's not too late." Salantha enforced commandingly.

Amalaka went silent, but doubt was very present in her eyes.

Gently, Shahaday said, "You haven't aged a day any more than the rest of us have. Ayayla has been the only one to increase in age these last twelve years and during this whole time not one of us has had our time of the month and well we know why that is. If our God can do that with us, then can He not do more so with even you, as well?"

Amalaka still looked about ready to object against what Shahaday was proposing, but Tagan sealed her lips shut, as he said, "Just believe."

Her eyes landed on him with shock. Slowly, she nodded and then standing up she quickly headed out of the fire's light and away from the others.

It seemed to be the signal to break up the meeting. Women split off in every direction, until only I and Tagan were left by the fire.

He was staring off in the darkness after where Amalaka had gone off to.

With wonder I whispered, "Do you really believe she can yet have a child?"

His warm gaze came to me, "It's happened before, so why not again?"

My eyes widened as I suddenly remembered a rather prominent Bible story.

Oh my!

Really?!

I looked outward toward where one of the three mothers I had been blessed with in life had disappeared off to. Oh how I wished for her sake that it would be so!

With a gasp I felt my focus suddenly being redirected as I was being pushed down flat onto the ground by the fire. All my air left me, as a very large and powerfully built male that had the most amazing eyes, came down over top of me gently.

I couldn't think, as I watched his lips come closer. Then a little desperately I squeaked out, "I thought....um..... I thought you weren't giving a tutorial on..... lovemaking....to...to the others?"

"What, this? No darling, this isn't love making." he said with evident humor, as his lips closed down over mine.

I don't know how much later it was when I felt the ability to breathe again, but it was a while. I opened my eyes to stare into his eyes that seemed to blaze with fire.

“You’re sure it's not?" I whispered.

“I'm sure.” He kissed me again and this time I stared into his eyes, as I gave as much as he did to the kiss.

Moving his lips off my own he kissed his way across my face in a way that made me feel each inch of the skin he touched was cherished by him. Breathlessly I whispered, even as my hands now clutched him to me, “Then what is it?”

His lips were back on mine then. Later, as if from a long distance away in which several centuries had passed by I heard him say, “Torment. This is sheer torment.”

I couldn't agree more with his statement.

I heard him whisper against my ear, “Want me to stop?”

Oh please no! My head turned and it was my lips that found his.

I suddenly didn't care about what anyone saw. Trustingly though, in the back part of my mind that could still reason, I knew that he did.

I was safe. I was also loved.

My lips drew back from his.

Smiling up at him I whispered, “I like torment.”

“You're very good at it." he said huskily.

“I am?”

“Oh yes!”

With a grin I whispered, “Do you want me to stop?”

“Honey, you would have to stop breathing to accomplish that and I don't ever want you to do that.”

The emotion in his voice was unfeigned, even as the sincerity of truth in his eyes melted my soul.

Laying wonderfully stretched out under the glorious weight of what had to be the most special man in the world I said even as tears leaked out of my eyes to spill into my hair, “You lied to me.”

His one brow hitched up higher, “I did? How?”

“This is lovemaking.”

He smiled then, even as his lips came back to mine.

Against them I felt his smile, even as he said, “I guess I did, but I'm not sorry.”

Neither was I.

I let my hands spear into his hair as I held him to me. If he could love me, then it was only in me to return the favor, even if it came at the cost of tormenting us both out of our minds.

~~~~~~~~~

Sytana

Sytana groaned and rolled over to face the other way from the kissing couple by the fire. She crammed her eyes shut with frustration though, as she could still hear them.

Her eyes opened and her private torment was distracted away from for a moment as she spied Ashandi sitting up not too far away. She was very interested in the scene taking place over by the fire.

Sytana watched her for a moment and Ashandi noticed her study of her. She flushed a little.

Sytana only smiled and said, "I know. It's hard not to watch."

Surprisingly. Ashandi nodded.

Carefully, Sytana said, "I'm here for you, if you ever want to talk about anything."

Ashandi glanced at her and then down. Sytana expected that to be the end of it, but to her surprise Ashandi spoke, "I really liked kissing. I….. it's a struggle….. not to. I…. I've wanted to…. to kiss you, especially out of all of the other women and…… do other things as well."

With that statement made Ashandi drew her knees up and buried her face against them.

Her head lifted though as Sytana softly said, "I know."

Ashandi looked at her with wet eyes that reflected her private shame.

Sytana met her gaze and said, "I'm very proud of you for not trying to do that with not only me, but with any of the others these last twelve years. You're not the only one among us that struggles with this."

Ashandi nodded emotionally and said, " I know, but….. I feel so wicked! I…. I should be better than this! I know better! I know God is real! I….. I want to please Him! I….. I still want what I had before though, too."

Salantha materialized out of the darkness. Ashandi gave a nervous start, but Salantha said nothing, just sat down right beside Ashandi and before she could move to pull back Salantha pulled her in against her side with an arm.

Ashandi lost it then. She started to sob and Salantha held her to her, combing her fingers soothingly through her long brown hair.

When Ashandi had quieted down a little Salantha brought her chin up and said, "You are not wicked. Say it."

"I… I'mmm nootttt …..wwwicked."

"That's right. You're just fighting a war. A long brutal war and in the end you're going to win. The real you is going to win."
~~~~~~~~~

"How do you know?"

"Because I know God is real, too. He's enough. He's enough for both of us."

Ashandi's eyes widened. She whispered, "You too?"

"Everyday."

Ashandi looked down, "I..... you're so strong though..... so righteous."

"I'm as weak as you are, when it comes down to what I want."

Ashandi, still staring at the ground said, "Why does knowing about your struggle make me feel better about my own?"

"Because you know you're not alone. I'm your friend and before long it will be us getting our faces kissed off - by a man."

Ashandi nodded.

Sytana sat down on Ashandi's other side and put her arm around her as well, "I'm your friend too."

Glancing over towards the couple alone by the fire she then said, "And I can hardly wait for the kissing either - by a man that is." Sytana quickly clarified.

Ashandi gave a watery chuckle and then softly admitted, "I'm kind of looking forward to it as well."

Seemingly of accord both she and Sytana glanced at Salantha. Salantha suddenly looked uncomfortable.

Mumbling, which was so unlike her, she said, "I am too, but......" leaving the rest unsaid, she gestured to the marred half of her face before bitterly adding, "what man would want to."

Sytana spoke, as if she couldn't believe her own ears, "You're beautiful! Any man who wouldn't kiss you would be out of his mind! I rebuke the whole notion that you think you're not attractive just because you have a few scars."

Ashandi spoke, "I second that. I didn't know you struggled with your appearance, but really you shouldn't. It's not that bad, really. I think it makes you look mysterious."

Salantha gave her a look.

"No really, it does."

Sytana nodded her head in back up affirmation of Ashandi's assertion.

Salantha looked down pensively before saying, "Well this is at least new, worrying about whether a man will find me attractive or not."

Ashandi squeezed knee consolingly, "Besides your mysterious face, what man could resist a woman that comes with her own lion pride. Did you see earlier that they are following us?"

Salantha nodded with a grin. She'd become very attached to the lions.

She'd been overjoyed to see them following along earlier in the day.

Shahaday came to sit down beside the three of them. Glancing curiously at them she asked, "So what are you guys talking about?"

Before Salantha or Ashandi could respond Sytana said, "Oh, nothing much. How long do you think they're going to keep this up?"

Entirely distracted, Shahaday glanced at the kissing couple that showed no signs of weakening. She gave a groan and said, "I don't know, but I wish they'd stop. I can't sleep with this going on."

The other three nodded, but the truth was that all four were more than fascinated to watch the scene by the fire take place.

Some things were better than sleep and this was one of them.

CHAPTER SIXTEEN

Distraction & Comfort

Two Days Later

Ayayla

I pulled my horse's reins up as Sytana abruptly stopped her mount just ahead of me. I had been mid column talking with Shahaday and now roughly half of us were stopped, while the other half continued on.

The others ahead of us abruptly stopped, as they noticed they weren't being followed. I pulled up alongside Sytana with concern, even as Salantha came racing up followed by Tagan.

Sytana was not looking at any of us. She was staring off to the West, even as we were headed to the North.

Though she was right here with us she seemed like she was miles away. Salantha made to speak, but Tagan gestured for her to remain quiet.

Long moments passed by and all of us waited anxiously. This was so unlike Sytana. She never caused a scene.

Seeming to come back from somewhere far off her head turned to Tagan. Her lips moved, "I have to go. I….. he needs me. I have to go….. now!"

Tagan nodded, "Then you need to go."

Looking incredulous, Salantha made to speak roughly in denial, but Sytana was already moving away.

Salantha wheeled about on her mount angrily, as all of us sat on our horses astounded by the blond's sudden unexpected action. I was stunned not only by Sytana, but Tagan as well.

How could he just let her go off by herself?!

It was virtually a death sentence!

I wanted to speak out, but I bit back my words. He must have a reason.

The man I had been coming to know had to have a reason for this.

Salantha was speaking, "I can't let her go off alone like this!"

My gaze left Sytana to fall on Tagan. He wasn't looking at either Sytana or Salantha, who was now almost beside herself. He was looking of all people at Ashandi.

Salantha was about to really cut loose, because of his inaction, when Ashandi spoke, "She won't be alone. I'll go with her."

Salantha wheeled around to face Ashandi, but she was already moving forward. She had to pass by Tagan on the way and when she did he held something out to her.

She took it from him questioningly.

"It's a map of where we are going. Whatever you do, don't let that fall into anyone else's hands."

Ashandi nodded and tucked it down the front of your shirt. Giving one last glance to Salantha she said, "I won't let anything happen to her."

Sounding very emotional Salantha said with passion, "You better not! I… you watch out for yourself, too."

Ashandi nodded and then she was cantering off down the slope after the lone rider. I had the very real worry that it might be the last that I ever saw of either of them.

Tagan looked about the group. Eyes left the two riders to view him.

"Right now is a hard moment for all of you. But you need to stop worrying, right now. As much as you all would like to keep that gentle soul safe you would always fail in one way or another. I say that because when you're called to a course of action by God the very safest you will ever be will be in doing what He has called you to do. She is safer out there right now than she would be here with us, because God wants her out there. By all means pray for her and Ashandi, but do not worry. They are both in God's hands and if it's His will, you will see them both again."

That said, he rode out the way we had been headed. One by one we followed, but we were all crying.

~~~~~~~~~

Sytana and Ashandi

Sytana looked to the side, as Ashandi pulled up beside her. Ashandi said nothing.

The two rode on for a while. Finally the blonde asked, "Did God tell you to come with me?"
~~~~~~~~~

"No, I don't.... I don't hear from Him as clearly as you do. Maybe one day."

"Why did you come then?"

"To keep your butt alive."

"I can defend myself!"

Ashandi simply nodded. The two rode on.

Sytana glanced at her again and biting her full lip she finally admitted, "Thank you for coming."

"What are friends for." Ashandi nonchalantly replied with, as if it was no real big thing to have left the group to come with her into the unknown.

"What if I get us both killed?"

"Well, in the advent of that, if it happens - you have my forgiveness now in advance."

They rode for two more hours during which Sytana took the lead. They were now in a forest.

An old forest with lots of understory growth. It would be very easy to get lost in such a place.

Despite that Ashandi was trying her best to memorize everything that could be called a landmark. The courage to come along, as well as the boldness of her usual demeanor, we're starting to wear off.

They were beyond vulnerable in this unknown setting. Trying not to let worry leach into her voice she called out as quietly as she could, "How do you know where to go?"

Sytana looked back, her already pale skinned complexion even now more pale than usual, "I don't."

"What?!" Ashandi squeaked out with.

"The horse just keeps walking." Sytana volunteered reluctantly.

"We're following the lead of a horse?!" Ashandi harshly whispered back.

"You can go back if you want to."

Ashandi abruptly rejected the notion of doing that. She was no coward.

This forest was creepy though. There weren't the sounds of birds that she was used to.

The place seemed dead somehow. No way on Earth was she leaving Sytana to face this place alone.

One thing was being made very clear to her. Sytana had more faith than she would ever have.

~~~~~~~~~
~~~~~~~~~

The Main Group Later That Evening

Ayayla

We all stared into the flames of the fire. No one spoke.

Tagan looked particularly morose. I was yet learning the way his mind worked, but it was obvious to me he was struggling with something.

As I studied him it came to me that he hadn't wanted to let them go.

Softly, I asked into the stillness, "How bad is it?"

He jerked slightly, and with reluctance he met my gaze and said, "It's bad. That whole section….. it's not good. I…… a few years ago I rescued a man from that region. I…. it was a trap. The man tried to kill me. I couldn't figure out why he would do that. There was no reason he should seek to kill me after nursing him back to life. It only dawned on me just before it was almost too late that I wasn't dealing with a man."

"It was a Borg? A human-looking Borg?" Shahaday breathed out with.

"No, but those do exist too. No, the man had a demon. Actually, he had several. Even with him half-dead I barely survived."

Salantha spoke, as we all watched the memories take place in Tagan's eyes as he gazed into the fire, "You killed him then?"

At virtually the same moment Shahaday said, "You used your technology to win?"

Tagan shook his head, "No, with the spiritual authority that I've been given through the Son of God I cast the demons out of the man. That man is now my closest friend. He wanted to come with me on this mission, but God said no. I don't think he would have let Sytana and Ashandi go off into that forest, as I did."

We were all silent for a moment. Shahaday was the one that spoke the thoughts of many, or at least mine, "Is there anything you can't do?"

Tagan looked up out of the fire at her with what looked almost like anger, but what I felt instead was pain. His voice raw sounding he said, "A great deal, actually. Like not stopping two women riding alone into hell!"

He stood up and left the fire light abruptly and reflexively I stood up too. I didn't know what to do.

Shahaday was speaking again, "Why couldn't he stop them, if that's what he wanted to do?"

I could have slapped her in that moment, instead I bit my lip and remained facing away from her.

Amalaka spoke, "Because God told him not to stop them. The man does whatever God says to do. It's not easy being a person of absolute faith. The more you know God the more you are held accountable for what you do by God. I watched him wake up out of a sound sleep last night. The rest of the night he drew up that map that he gave to Ashandi today. He did all he could do to help them that was permitted of him and yet he has a good heart and it's eating him alive right now, because he thinks he failed to do the right thing."

I started forward into the dark, even as Amalaka said, "Ayayla, you should go to him. He's at his weakest right now. He needs both distraction and comfort."

~~~~~~~~~

Salantha shook her head as she watched Ayayla disappear and asked Amalaka, "How do you know so much about men? You were just a young girl when your father was taken from you."

Amalaka shook her head, "I honestly don't know. It just comes to me. As curious as you all might be, leave them alone tonight."

No one by the fire had any other intention to start out with, but if they'd had it - it was now squashed.

Amalaka reached out her hands to those to the side of her and said, "Those who are willing, let us pray for Sytana and Ashandi together as one."

In unison all those gathered linked hands as all the women prayed for the ones that were not with them for the first time in their lives.

~~~~~~~~~

Ayayla

I found him in the moonlight with his head pressed up against a tree, even as his hands gripped it, as if ready to do battle with it. Coming closer I put my arms around him in a silent hug.

He stiffened, but made no protest. I could feel it - the war vibrating around inside of him.

I had to stop it. I had to bring peace, as I couldn't bear to watch him tear himself apart.

Bitterly, he said, "They don't have a chance!"

Pulling at his waist I turned him, which only happened because he let me.

Meeting his troubled eyes I said softly, "That's not what you said earlier today. You said they couldn't be safer, because they were where God wanted them to be."

"That was then. It's what the others wanted to hear."

"That's not the truth and we both know it."

"They are my responsibility and I let them go! Do you have any idea how rare a good woman is?! I just let two of them join the ranks of the dead, as if there weren't enough already gone from this life! They can't be replaced!!!"

I put my hand in the center of his heaving chest. His turbulent gaze came back to me as if drawn to me by some unseen force.

"First off you obeyed God. You are not at fault for their decision to leave. You did all you could to help them by giving them that map that I bet God didn't tell you to make. Second, not one of these women is your responsibility except for me. They have all chosen to follow you, but I've chosen to be with you forever."

I withdrew my hand and before he could act I pulled my shirt up and over my head and tossed it to the side. His breath hissed out, even as he pressed back against the tree behind him.

He had nowhere to go. He was trapped.

I unclasped my skirt and let it fall.

"Now is not the time!" He gritted out angrily.

Instead of answering him directly I said, "I'll put my clothes back on if you ask me to."

His lips remained closed and then I made sure they stayed that way by leaning up to kiss him passionately. His hands gripped down about my bare waist and I knew the intent was to pull me back from him, but strangely they seemed to lack all strength to do so.

All he could manage to do was pull his head back from mine. His voice husky sounding he said with what sounded a lot like desperation, "You don't know what you're doing!"

Oh, but I did. I suddenly knew exactly what I was to be doing.

As strong as he was he had no chance against the need I had been created to fulfill. Looping my arms about his neck I smiled into his eyes, even as I kissed him again.

This man was mine. He wasn't going anywhere or thinking about anything but me for the rest of the night.

He needed this distraction and my desire was to comfort him. The troubles of this life might return with a vengeance in the morning, but for now I was going to be the haven that he could find a moment of peace in.

Groaning against my lips he gave up the fight and I won everything. It's what I had thought I wanted, but in truth all I was focused on in the moment was loving him.

~~~~~~~~~

Ashandi and Sytana

Sytana shivered uncontrollably. Most of it wasn't from the falling rain, but rather from emotion.

The horses were dead.

The night was alive with the sound of them being torn into and devoured down below. Thirty feet up a large tree and out on a large branch both women sat back to back with their swords in their hands, as they waited for it to be their turn to be devoured.

They had barely made it up the tree. Sytana knew she wouldn't have survived the attack, if it hadn't been for the smaller brunette.

The girl had the reflexes of a cat and had launched out of her own saddle to knock Sytana out of hers just as some beast had launched from the darkened understory foliage.

Ashandi's arm has been deeply scratched by a branch in the fall, but using the horses as a distraction she'd pushed the blonde toward a tree and made her go up first. The horses hadn't had a chance, but at least they had served one last duty of buying them the time needed to climb up to a defensible position.

It was utterly dark now, but they could still hear what was taking place down below. Soon their horses' fate would be theirs too.

A cold rain had started to fall an hour ago. Crying, even as she gripped her sword Sytana said, " I am so sorry! I..... I was told to go to him. I ......I am so sorry! I...."

"Shut up."

There was a moment of silence other than for the sound of flesh being ripped apart down below.

Trying to keep her voice modulated, Ashandi said, "Tomorrow you are just going to have to lead us instead of your horse doing all the work."

Sytana half turned her head with incredulousness, but she couldn't see anything in the dark. Her shoulders firmed then and her grip on the sword got tighter.

On the other side of her Ashandi had no such new-found faith in the moment to indwell courage from. She'd just said that to make the other woman feel better.
~~~~~~~~~

Staring at the bole of the tree not that far from her she gripped her sword and waited. She may well die this night, but Sytana would live.

No matter what, Sytana would live. Of the two of them, by Ashandi's reckoning, Sytana deserved the most to keep on living.

She blinked the water off her long eyelashes. She heard the sliding grip of a claw on wet tree bark.

Unaware of the immediate threat Sytana called out loudly over the rain, "I think this predator is possessed. Why else would it attack us given how they have been our friends over the last twelve years."

Ashandi, to herself made the mental note of that as a possible, '*Could Be*', but just the same - this thing was dying tonight. She swung her sword.

Blood showered everywhere, even as a gagged sounding cry of pain sounded out. There was a loud thump, as the predator collided with the forest floor below.

Suddenly; however, there was something trying to get into her. There was really no other way to explain it.

Whatever it was - it was something far worse than the dead predator lying below.

Ashandi dropped her sword and scratched at her own skin as a cry of fright bubbled up out of her lips, as she felt herself choked about the neck by a grip she couldn't shake off.

It wasn't her scratching hands that saved her though. Another hand reached over her shoulder and seized about something invisible.

Ashandi could suddenly breathe again and as she gasped for air, Sytana's voice came out into the night with death laden passion, "You can't have her hellspawn. She's my friend. I rebuke you for your attack upon us in the name of the Creator's Son, Jesus Christ."

The dark mass bound up by her hand seemed to writhe and then it exploded with a brief burst of light as Sytana - now out for blood said, "I command you to be put to death."

Both women jumped at the flash of color that occurred then. The rain stopped.

Shaking, Ashandi pressed back against Sytana's arms that we're now consolingly wrapped about her.

Her voice sounding a little high-pitched, Ashandi asked, "Did you just kill a demon?"

"I..... I think so."

Ashandi pressed back more resolutely, as she whispered, "Thank you."

Sytana started to speak, but Ashandi squeezed her arm and said, "Don't you dare apologize again."

"I.... no..... I was just going to say that I dropped my sword."

"Oh.... yeah, I did too, but that's all right."

"How do you figure that?" Sytana asked doubtfully.

With a little of her usual bravado returning the brunette said, "What? You're kidding, right? Every demon in this forest is shaking in a hole right now with a Demon Slayer such as yourself on the loose."

"I......ah.... well, I just said the words."

"No, it's more than that. You believe the words and....... if I doubted them before, I don't now."

Both women remained clasped together both in terms of the need for warmth and a newly forged bond out of having both saved each other's lives this night.

CHAPTER SEVENTEEN

The Evil One

Ayayla

Tagan looked back at me concernedly for what must have been the fiftieth time. As with every time previous I just smiled at him by way of reply.

There was no way I was letting him know how tired I was or sore for that matter. Last night had been the best night of my life and yet I was paying the price for it now.

For at least the 20th time today another of the women drew up alongside of me and holding up a hand to forestall conversation I said, "No, I am not talking about it, other than to say that it was wonderful and something that you're well off waiting for."

The woman closed her open mouth with a sigh, only to then plead. "You won't tell us anything, Ayayla?"

I shook my head, "No, it's personal and besides that, I don't have his permission to talk about it."

She nodded and drifted off just as so many of the others had done so today.

"That was a very good answer I think." Amalaka said approvingly from my other side.

Glancing at me worriedly though she asked, "Did you get any sleep at all?"

Biting my lip for a moment I delayed, but then admitted, since she was my mother in a way, "I passed out a couple of times."

Oh, the look she gave me then.

"What? You're the one that said to distract him."

Nodding her head slowly, she admitted, "Yes, yes I did."

I shifted uncomfortably on the saddle, she glanced at me again and I let the truth slip out, "Being tired isn't what has me about to fall out of this saddle though."

Her lips firmed.

Oh no! I knew that look.

She abruptly rode ahead. Silently, I screamed inside for her to come back.

She stopped beside Tagan. They were too far away to hear.

I could only imagine what she was saying to him. I saw Tagan nod after a moment.

He then pointed something out to Salantha and then he was riding back toward me. Oh this was truly embarrassing!

Smiling riders sped up, until we were the last two riders in the column. I was on the verge of opening my mouth to state that I had not been complaining about anything, when he said, “You look really tired and uncomfortable.”

My mouth abruptly closed. In truth, I was both.

“Want to come over here?”

I would, but the back of his horse hardly had anything to offer in terms of comfort.

“Not back there silly, up here.”

I glanced at his arms. I bit my lip.

He made the choice for me. Lifting me up and over I found myself sitting sideways in front of him.

His one arm was behind me and well - he made the position comfortable somehow. I trusted him completely not to drop me.

My eyes closed in part, because I was tired, but also because I didn't want to see all of the smiling looks that we were getting.

Tiredly, I said, “Won’t your arm get tired?”

“Like I care if it does, honey. Go to sleep.”

“If you get tired just put me back on my horse.” I said.

“Sure.” he said.

I knew he wouldn't though. He’d probably let his arm fall off first.

If I hadn't known enough about him before last night I now most certainly did. He was amazing and if I let him he would spoil me rotten.

Smiling, I cuddled into him and fell asleep in his arms in the middle of the day.

Riders further up the column all turned forward in their saddles and sighed longingly.

Amalaka just shook her head, only Salantha seemed distant from the tender moment that was transpiring. Her brow seemed permanently creased with worry, but she said nothing.

“They made it through the night.”

Salantha jumped slightly at Amalaka’s words.

She glanced at Amalaka and asked, “How do you know?”

"Just do."

"What about tonight, though?" Salantha asked.

"One day at a time. One day is all we really have anyway. That aside, you seem to be forgetting the promise that all you women that went in search of Ayayla's parents received from the Most High."

Salantha blinked and then softly she admitted, "I guess I did."

Some time passed by and during that time Salantha began to breathe easier. Glancing over at Amalaka she said, "Thank you for reminding me."

"What are good friends for, if not to help us when we need it most."

Salantha nodded in return. It was the truth.

Ashandi and Sytana

Ashandi kept as low to the ground as she could. They had been walking for hours.

At first Sytana had been in the lead, but now it was Ashandi. She was feeling a definite pull of some kind.

It was hard to define. Wordlessly the two women glanced at each other as they felt compelled to go in the exact same direction as each other.

Did they both have the same fate of belonging to one man?

Finally, Sytana, put words to the silent struggle going on, "I don't think so."

They both knew what she meant. Exasperated sounding Ashandi exclaimed back, "Then how can you explain how I feel? I can feel him now too!"

Sytana gave a helpless shrug and repeated, "I don't know, but I don't think so. There's something we're not seeing"

"I don't want to steal your man!" Ashandi said, with emotional passion, even as inwardly she quaked with the realization of how much she suddenly wanted to be with a man.

Sytana spoke, "If it is as you think it is it's not stealing, not if I willingly share him with you."

Ashandi just shook her head no. Sytana would give a stranger the shirt off her back.

There was simply no way she was going to butt into her relationship with a man. The realization of the line she wasn't going to cross brought a hint of pain, because it meant she might have to do without having a man herself.

Why did that suddenly matter so much to her?

Both women abruptly froze then, as they heard a groan. They were in a very rocky area with drop-offs everywhere.

They had left the forest behind mid-morning and for the last two hours had been making their way through the uneven rocky terrain.

Not daring to breathe both women remained completely still. There was another groan.

Both women turned slightly and started creeping forward across the boulder-strewn ground. Coming to the edge of a ledge they peered over it.

Sytana gasped loudly. The man, and it very much was a man, glanced up at them out of the depression that he lay in.

It was obvious that his leg was badly broken. That wasn't all.

There was an arrow shaft buried in his one shoulder.

Sytana did not hesitate. She was up and climbing over the edge in an instant.

"Sytana, no! Wait!" Ashandi called-out warningly, but Sytana would not hear it.

Ashandi scrambled down after her hurriedly. Something was wrong about the man.

He was beautiful, if you could consider a man to be so, but he ...... he just wasn't the right one.

Deeply confused Ashandi hurried up to Sytana, even as the man feverishly lifted himself up to prop himself back against a boulder. His hand fumbled for something nearby and Ashandi saw that it was a short throwing spear.

She full on clutched onto Sytana then, but the blonde started to drag her.

Desperately, Ashandi tried to break through, "Sytana for pity's sake, stop! He has a weapon! He thinks you're one of them! One of the other women!"

Sytana paused.

"Look at the arrow. A female colony made that. I've seen similar ones like it before. If you go any closer he will kill you!"

Sytana gave her a look then that had Ashandi releasing her. With soft confidence she spoke, "No, he won't."

Ashandi didn't know how or why, but she believed her.

Sytana turned to the man. She pulled her sword out.

The man lifted the spear. Sytana laid her sword on the ground.

Next she laid down her knife. Pulling her water jug up she shook the water in it slightly.

Slowly then, she started moving closer to the man. The spear lifted and as it did Ashandi helplessly twisted her hands together, as if they were bound from coming to the aid of her friend.

Slowly. Sytana got down on her knees. With all her focus on the man she said, "I will not hurt you. I promise!"

The man's eyes showed no sign of recognition of her words.

Warningly Ashandi called-out, "I don't think he can understand us."

Sytana nodded, but continued onward anyway. The short spear came up, until the point was against Sytana's throat.

She didn't stop though. Swallowing nervously, against the point of the spear she drew close enough to be able to reach the now open jug out to touch the man's lips.

His eyes were on hers and hers on his as she tilted the jug up.

The man drank heavily from it. It must have been a long time since he'd had anything to drink.

The spear collapsed back to the ground, even though the wild look of wary distrust had not left his eyes. Sytana continued to hold the jug for him.

Looking beyond exhausted, the man at last stopped drinking. Sytana set the jug off to the side within reach of the man.

Very slowly, she moved her fingers to his shoulder that had the arrow shaft buried in it. Making all her movements agonizingly slow and non-threatening she slowly tore the rip in the bloody homespun cloth wider.

She surveyed the wound for a moment and then looking very pale she glanced back at Ashandi, "I think it was poisoned."

Ashandi nodded. That fit with what she knew about other colonies that specifically focused on hunting men down like it was some kind of trophy hunt competition.

The man, shot with the arrow and poisoned by its effects, had stumbled over this drop-off and broken his leg. Without their help he was dead.

Even with their help he might not make it. Ashandi started moving closer.

The man re-gripped the spear again. Hurriedly, Ashandi divested herself of all of her weapons.

The man's hand remained on the spear. Dry mouthed, Ashandi drew closer.

Coming to his leg she made a decision. He may not understand their language, but the leg needed to be fixed.

She felt gently at the break. It wasn't as bad as she had first thought.

She glanced up. He was watching her.

He really was handsome, but there was just something off about him.

Pointing to his leg she then pointed at his spear. He understood.

It was clear he understood by the look in his eye, but he did nothing. Then slowly, he brought the spear up.

Ashandi stopped breathing. Instead of having the point of it jammed through her throat though, he handed it out to her.

She took it from him very carefully. Standing up she put her weight against the middle of it with her foot and snapped it in half.

Kneeling back down she laid the pieces to the side. She glanced up.

He met her gaze. He gave a slight nod.

Gripping his leg she inwardly winced, as she jerked it hard in the way it needed to go. The bone clicked together audibly and both women cried out reflexively, because they felt the pain of the action dearly.

They'd made more noise than he had. He was sweating profusely now though.

Quickly, Ashandi went about securing his leg to the broken spear with some leather string she always carried. It wasn't the first broken appendage that she had assisted in securing, but it was certainly the largest.

Men were big!

Wiping at her brow, even as Sytana mopped at his face she finished up her work. Moving up higher she changed places with Sytana, who went to the other side of the man.

Gently, she pulled on his shoulder slightly to bring him away from the boulder he was resting back against. The arrow hadn't gone all the way through, but it was close to it.

Glancing over at an anxious Sytana, she said, " I think the best thing will be to push it on through. We will first break this end off and then push and pull it the rest of the way through."

Sytana looked like she was on the verge of throwing up. Ashandi didn't feel so good about it either, but something had to be done.

Glancing down to the man she tried to replicate with her hands what she intended to do. He nodded.

"Get me some of that rock moss. We'll pack the wounds with it and it might help draw out some of the poison."

Sytana quickly complied. Preparations made and with sweat now rolling off of her, Ashandi readied herself to perform the task.

Sytana was back on the same side as she was. Hands poised on the arrow shaft Ashandi looked into the man's feverish eyes and whispered, "I'm sorry."

She snapped the fletching off the back of the arrow and tried to ignore how his whole body jolted. Picking up a flat rock with her hand on the other side of it she smashed it down hard on the end of the broken arrow shaft.

The arrow point tore through his back along with some of the shaft. Blood was everywhere, both women were crying and the man was groaning, even as he clutched hard enough at a rock to leave a hand impression on it.

Ashandi's blood-drenched hands gripped about the shaft behind his back and she pulled hard. His deep groan became a shout.

He abruptly jerked and then passed out cold. Ashandi threw the arrow to the side - blood was everywhere.

Sytana was almost beside herself, "We've killed him!"

Ashandi eased the unconscious man over onto his side. Meeting Sytana's terror-stricken eyes, she said, "No, you have not. He's not going to die. I promise!"

Quickly, she packed both ends of the wound with copious amounts of the rock moss. Ripping up the rest of the man's shirt she began to tie it off tightly over the moss.

With that done she shakily let Sytana take over. Crawling away several feet she sat back against a boulder.

She was covered in blood, but what attracted her attention was the sight of Sytana resting the man's head on her lap. She was praying over the man as if her life depended on it and not his.

Ashandi smiled softly at the sight. There was nothing to worry about now, but just the same she closed her own eyes and whispered out her own prayer for her friend's man.

That was just the beginning of the two women's struggle to keep the man alive. In the two days that followed the man shook and trembled in the grips of a terrible fever.

Both women exhausted themselves trying to keep him still so that he wouldn't hurt himself. Amazingly, the wound itself did not become infected, but the poison in his system raged like a fire.

On the morning of the third day Sytana opened her eyes wearily. She glanced down in fear, as she always did, in half expectation that the man might have died while she slept.

Instead of death she saw life. His eyes were open and clear.

His head was in her lap and he was just quietly laying there regarding her. Sytana blushed brightly.

The man, whose features were more of a darker olive tan color in complexion, became visibly intrigued.

"I think he likes what he sees." Ashandi said good-humoredly from a few feet away.

The man had been awake for an hour. He'd never once looked at her, just Sytana.

Sytana glanced at Ashandi as the latter got up off the ground.

"I'm going to go see if I can get us something to eat."

Sytana nodded, and swiftly her eyes were back on the man, as if she found them to be enthralling in some way.

Smiling, Ashandi left the two to be together alone. He was definitely Sytana's man.

Moving across the rocky terrain Ashandi made for a bordering fringe of trees. Reaching the trees she discovered it to be but the beginning of a sharply down sloped area.

Moving downhill through the trees towards the pool of water at the base of the gorge she abruptly stopped and then flattened down behind a boulder. There were three women further down the slope.

They were weathered looking old hags to be sure. Slowly, Ashandi reached down and pulled her sword free.

If the three old women kept coming this way she would kill them, but she had to be careful, because all three of them had bows at the ready.

One of them cackled about something and Ashandi winced. Would she have turned into one of those old hags hunting down the rest of mankind if she had chosen to leave the colony that night long ago now in the past?

The odds were alarmingly high. She'd made the right decision, even if there was no man for her.

She jumped startled then, as the ground around the old women abruptly swirled with action. All three old women fell slain as a number of men stood up out of concealment so clever that Ashandi hadn't even suspected that they were there.

She had to get back and warn Sytana!

Almost on the heels of that thought a big hand closed over her mouth, even as another grasped about the wrist that held her sword. Ashandi tried to fight, but the hand over her mouth wouldn't budge, even as the hand at her wrist was crushing her.

The sword fell with a clang to the rocks. Whoever her assailant was stood up and Ashandi's feet no longer touched the ground.

She flailed about kicking and hitting like her life depended on it, because it likely did. Out of the corner of her eye she saw the incoming fist.

She tried to turn away, but in the end she was helpless to avoid its heavy impact. She went limp as she saw stars bloom across the horizon of her vision everywhere.

Hanging like a doll in her captor's arms her eyes rolled around in her head. Then for a brief moment her vision cleared enough to see the man who had captured her.

He had to be the identical twin to Sytana's man!

Only one thing was noticeably different, other than for the fact this one looked noticeably meaner than the other one. He had a scar that went down the middle of one half of his face.

The evil twin had her at his complete mercy. With a moan of despair Ashandi passed out completely.

Sytana looked up as she heard noise. Seven men were closing in on her and one of them was carrying Ashandi.

There was nothing to be done, even if she could have tried to. The odds were just too great.

A hand closed over hers reassuringly. Her scared eyes met the man's eyes, whose head still lay in her lap.

There was a calming assurance in them towards her, but it wasn't much to go on. She gasped then, as she got a better look at the man holding Ashandi.

He none too gently let Ashandi slide down to the ground and in the next moment he was right beside her and speaking with what had to be his twin brother.

The Brothers

"Arn, you are well?"

"I will be, thanks to her and the other one, Vorin."

Vorin's eyes drifted up to the very shocked looking blonde, whose lap held his brother's head. The woman was beyond attractive and yet the feisty little brunette held his fascination more.

"What strange company you keep, brother."

Arn instead of responding with humor reached out to grip his brother's hand and say, "Don't let any harm come to them! They saved me. They were not the ones who hunted me."

"I will try, but you know how Vorsitch is."

"I don't care how Vorsitch is, try harder!" Arn forcefully commanded. He was the older of the two by a few minutes, but Vorin was the more deadly, while his brother was the peacemaker.

Such unbridled passion as this from his brother was unusual for Vorin to see. It was clear that he was clearly taken in by the blonde.

Who wouldn't be?

Vorsitch, the group leader, knelt down, "It is good to see you alive, Arn! We thought you dead from the poison of those witches. Speaking of witches, who are these two?" He asked, suspiciously.

"They are not witches. That is all I can tell you of them."

"I'll be the judge of that." Vorsitch said dismissively.

Ashandi rubbed at her jaw. She and Sytana were being held under the guard of two of the men and away from the others. Sytana's man was putting up quite the effort in their defense it would seem.

The apparent leader, a big looking brute, wasn't happy about it either. Their voices grew more animated by the moment.

The leader leaned in yelling a bit closer at the brother on the ground and almost immediately the evil twin squatted down beside his brother's head. The leader abruptly backed off in his verbal assault of the other.

"I don't like him." Sytana said, with quiet passion, in reference to the yelling leader.

Ashandi grunted her ascent before adding, "I think the feeling is mutual."

The leader abruptly got up and came toward the two women shadowed along by the twin brother as he did so. To the women's surprise the leader spoke haltingly in their language, "Who are you and why are you yet so young in appearance?"

Before Sytana could speak Ashandi spoke, "It's none of your business who we are and as for our age that is also our business and not yours."

Without warning the man's hand swung out in a backhanded slap that caught her across the face and sent her falling backward several paces. Sytana started forward, but Ashandi pushed her back.

Staring into the leader's face she faced him head-on without any sign of fear to be discerned. The man looked like he was literally itching to kill them.

Glancing to Sytana he then asked quite the unexpected question of, "You are a virgin."

Sytana blushed the brightest of reds. In some ways her propensity for blushing was its own lie detector test.

The man nodded, "You at least have some hope of redemption. You may live, but you - I can tell that you're one of them!"

His hand reached for a knife at his waist. The action was halted by the twin brother.

Ashandi glanced up at his scarred unsmiling face. Maybe he wasn't so evil, but then was he any good either?

Vorin

"You are not killing her. It is not honorable."

Vorsitch seemed to explode and aggressively got up into his face to shout, "Who are you to lecture me on honor! You've killed more of the witches than anyone!"

Vorin's gaze did not relent nor did his voice rise in volume as he said, "I have only killed those who sought to kill me, as for these two women they are clearly different. Whoever heard of a virgin witch and as for the brown haired one she set my brother's leg and freed the arrow from his body. Those are not the actions of an enemy."

"You saw the guilt on her face! She's one of them!"

"So what if she is. There's no rule that says we have to be like them and kill every one of them that we come across as they seek to do to us."

"Her kind just very nearly killed your brother! Do you not care about this?"

"She was not one of the attackers. She has done nothing worthy of death. My brother wants her to remain alive along with the blonde."

"Well, I'm the one who is in charge, not your brother!"

Vorin remained silent, even as silence was often his way where his brother was far more outgoing with his speech. He was at his most deadly when he was quiet.

Vorsitch seemed to sense that and abruptly changed tactics. "Fine. I will not kill her. Instead, let us let nature do the testing for us as to whether she is worthy to live or not. There is a rocky cliff nearby here. I have climbed it in the past. It is doable, but not easy. If she reaches the top of the cliff she is free to go. If she doesn't then she dies."

Vorin stared at him quietly, as the other men of the group reluctantly nodded in that it seemed like a fair compromise. Vorin continued to say nothing as the brunette was roughly pulled up to her feet and hustled along by Vorsitch and the others.

The blonde, her eyes full of worry, made to follow, but Vorin grabbed her arm and pointed towards his brother, who was straining to see what was going on. Her eyes turned from the wounded man to follow after her friend, who was being roughly led away.

Then, she turned her gaze back to Vorin and lifting her hands she folded them together and said a single word, even as tears streamed from her eyes. She was clearly begging him to intercede on behalf of her friend.

There was nothing but the most sincerest of emotions in her gaze. He nodded slightly.

Then pointing at his brother again he headed off after the others. He didn't know what Vorsitch was up to, but he didn't like the feeling he had about what was about to take place at all.

These women were different. The event of them should be applauded - not punished.

Reaching the base of the cliff where the others were gathered he looked up. It looked to be an impossible climb.

Vorsitch spoke to the woman in her language. Looking shaken of heart she glanced up at the cliff beyond her.

Then, of all things, she glanced at him imploringly.

Vorsitch prodded her toward the cliff and at the edge of a knife she turned away and quickly started to climb.

Vorin watched for a while.

Vorsitch ordered the others to kill her if she tried to come back down. There were only a few hours of daylight left as it was.

The girl truly was doing well, but….. the climb looked impossible.

Vorin left the scene swiftly.

CHAPTER EIGHTEEN

God Knew

Ashandi drug herself up over another almost clear expanse of rock face. She'd had only the barest of finger holds to manage by, but somehow she had made it up.

The task at first had seemed impossible, but amazingly she had made it three quarters of the way up the cliff. That said, she was not an optimistic type of person.

It was starting to get dark and every muscle in her body was beyond exhausted. It was a real temptation to just rest on the ledge that she was on, but with a groan she forced herself to get back up and start climbing again.

Her life, maybe even Sytana's depended on it. Wearily, she started to make her way up the last expanse of cliff face.

The evil twin, and yes he was most definitely evil, had just stood there and done nothing to intercede!

"Scarred face, my foot! I wouldn't have that man if he was the last one on earth!" she exclaimed righteously, even as the anger she felt within helped to renew her energy to continue in the task that she was at.

Her fingers were bleeding after another thirty minutes of continuous climbing. She pulled herself up over another ledge.

It was getting dark and cold. Very cold.

Opening her eyes she took in the last twenty or so feet to the top of the cliff. Feeling a sudden alarm at what she saw she stood up.

The last part of the cliff was absolutely sheer. There was not so much as a crack or projection of any kind to grab a hold of.

Panicked, she made her way all along the ledge, but it was the same everywhere. She almost tripped over something.

Looking down she saw a human skeleton. It was a female.

Everything went still inside at the sight of the bleached bones. This had all been a trap. An evil game.

There was no way up. If she went back down they would kill her.

She didn't even think she had the strength to go back down. Sinking down with her back to the cliff she felt the release of emotion she'd been battling for hours finally let loose. "Why God?!" She sobbed out.

"Don't You love me? Am I to tarnished for You? I trusted You! I waited! I said no to everything! I….." feeling that words were at a complete lack of use to express what she needed to she stopped and simply balled with unrepressed emotion against her drawn up knees.

She was going to die and Sytana was going to be left alone with these awful men. It wasn't fair!

She jerked, as something gently bumped into her hair.

Startled, she looked up from her knees and peered out into the gloom of early evening.

It was a rope!

Holding her breath she got up and craning her head back she followed it up the rest of the way to the top of the cliff. The evil twin was there holding the other end of it.

Patiently, he shook the rope slightly. Her mouth dry, Ashandi stared at him.

He had the scar and now he was offering to pull her up. Her mind traced back over the words Ayayla had said.

She was supposed to climb. She glanced down the dizzying distance that she had managed to come up all on her own by. She had climbed.

She'd climbed until it was impossible to climb any further. It hit her then.

God had known that this moment would happen long before it actually had!

She hadn't quit. She'd done what she was told to do.

Now….. now it was time to be pulled up to safety…… by the man with the scar.

Ashandi closed her eyes.

This was it. This was her moment of faith. Her chance to be like Sytana if for only a moment.

Opening her eyes she focused on the rope that was still there before her face. Taking it in hand she wrapped it about herself, as she felt like she was too weak to trust herself to hold on to it with just her hands.

Abruptly, once she was secured off, she started being lifted up the side of the cliff. Closing her eyes she imagined the sudden slackness that would herald the moment that the evil twin let go of the rope.

It didn't happen though. Instead she felt his hands.

They untied the rope and then when she stumbled they were carrying her. For the first time in her life she truly felt what it was like to be held by a man.

Her senses picked up on that they were suddenly somewhere much darker and with the advent of that the man set her down on the ground. There was noise and then a spark and then flames were rising.

Ashandi watched as he made a rather large fire at the mouth of the cave. She sat there not knowing what to expect, but it wasn't him coming back to her and picking her up as if she was a small child and setting her down on his lap.

Granted she wasn't all that big, but still she started to try to sit up only to receive a sharp glance from him that stopped any further movement on her part. Apparently, he really wanted to hold her, which was sort of alright as he was so very warm.

As the minutes went by all the chill left her bones as he held her there saying nothing. He seemed to be saying a lot in a way though.

In fact, this unexpected tenderness was almost like an apology. He said something then.

Ashandi didn't need a translator to know what he'd said. He'd actually apologized.

He hadn't known about the cliff being a trap. He wasn't the sort to do that kind of thing to someone.

She didn't know how she knew that but she did. Maybe he wasn't so evil after all.

The scar on his face certainly made him wicked looking though. Ashandi shifted in his hold.

She needed distance all of a sudden. If she didn't get away - like right now - something bad might happen.

His hands were moving then, but instead of letting her go she found herself straddling his lap with his wickedly good looking face right before her. She blinked and that was about all she had time for before his hands speared into the long brown tresses of her hair and anchored her head still as he mashed his lips passionately against hers.

Her thighs gripped about his waist, even as her hands hovered out in mid air as if unsure of what to do. This was ….. this was so…… amazing!

Slowly, her hands touched his face and then slid into his hair, as he did one of her most favorite things ever by simply kissing her. She loved kissing.

That said she'd never ever been kissed like this. He did it better - much better than anyone else ever had.

He was so vastly different from his brother despite the uncanny resemblance. Suddenly feeling aggressive she tried to kiss him back more passionately than he was kissing her, but that soon proved impossible.

After a few moments of heated passionate struggle she surrendered with a moan and let him have his way with her.

He was the one.

CHAPTER NINETEEN

The Map

Ashandi's eyes flickered. It was so bright!

It must be morning. Her eyes abruptly slammed open.

Oh my!

Her hand had already gone to her lips. Abstractly, despite her burgeoning panic, she immediately noticed a greenish paste that had been dried to her skin, where her hands had been cut from the climb up the cliff.

Bringing her hand further to her nose she sniffed and recognized the same herbal compounds that she would have used for a minor cut. The thing was she hadn't done this.

Her eyes closed as her awakened senses told her that she was completely bare of clothing. Biting her lip she forced herself to remember everything, as if she would ever forget.

After a few long moments of heavy breathing her eyes opened and slowly she glanced around the cave entrance. He was nowhere in sight, but she felt him. He was near.

Hurriedly, she sat up her face awash with color. All her clothes were beneath her along with his shirt.

Her eyes closed again. It had all really actually happened.

It hadn't been a dream. Her eyes opening she quickly went about getting dressed.

She tried not to focus on how her body felt, but it was hard. She felt alive almost as if she'd been unlocked from some prison.

Biting her lip almost to the point of bleeding she paused now that she was fully dressed. Stooping down she picked up his shirt.

It was in rough condition, barely serviceable as an article of clothing. She could make a better shirt than this.

Last night, other than for the apology, he hadn't said a word. He was so quiet.

She liked to talk, to argue, even verbally fight, but he just gazed at you out of those hazel eyes and spoke volumes without a word spoken.

He had not used her last night. Far from it actually.

Her hand lifted up to wipe at sudden tears. Whispering softly she said, “Thank You, God. I would have been dead yesterday if it wasn't for You. You even provided him. I.... I thought he was mean..... he's just quiet and .... serious. I.... I like him.”

Looking up she confessed more loudly, “I like the man that You've given me to, but.... I'm scared now..... was..... was last night the same for him as it was for me?”

There didn't seem to be an answer to that, but there was a pressing revelation that did come to mind. Her hand slapped at her shirt over top of her full breasts - the map!

Vainly, she looked about on the floor of the cave. It wasn't there.

She turned to the cave entrance. There was only one conclusion to be had - he had it.

Vorin

A map like this should never have been made. The realities it contained within it were simply too dangerous, if it were to fall into the wrong hands.

That said, he analyzed every facet of its detail. Among other gifts he had the gift of remembering everything he saw with perfect recollection.

As much as it was a gift it was also a curse, as there were many things he wished he could forget. He glanced up over the edge of the leather that the map had been drawn out on.

Everything brightened at the sight of her. Last night was something that he never wanted to forget.

Had it been the same for her? He felt sure that it had, but now; she was coming towards him with the most trepidatious look on her pretty face.

As completely unsettled as he knew her to be, he chose only to register the reality of how cute she was. With huge questioning eyes she came to a stop.

He noticed his shirt was folded over her arm. That was nice of her.

At first he had thought her to be a bit of a brat, but last night he had simply realized that she was just a passionate woman. Very passionate, but then so was he - he just chose to never show it to most people.

He had to her though. It had almost seemed like it had been demanded of him by her.

Like being with her made him interact with life more intimately. He didn't know what she thought her plans were for today or for that matter the rest of her life, but she could throw them all out.

She was his, permanently.

She looked a bit choked up and it was clear that she was finding it hard to speak. That was surprising as last night she'd been one unending song of vocal delight.

The memory of last night forced his lips to twitch into a soft smile. He strangely didn't mind letting her see that she'd made an impact on him.

She hadn't kept anything back from him last night so why should he in regards to her. Also he didn't want her to be afraid of him.

Whether he liked it or not most people were, except for his brother. He very much didn't want her to be afraid though.

Her eyes were on his lips. She blinked and seemed to visibly force them away from that aspect of him and back up to meet his own gaze.

Her lips moved and a single word came out of her lips as she pointed at the map in his hands. The word though unfamiliar must be the word for '*please*'.

She knew how important the information on this map was clearly. That said, he didn't think she'd been the one to draw it.

She was clearly under orders to protect it. What to do?

She hadn't seen him remove it last night when he had undressed her. In all reality that was probably the safest place for the map, because no one - no one - was going to ever see her breasts, but him.

Casually, he folded the map up, until it was once again a slim profile. Her eyes watched him closely the whole time.

Lifting a hand he crooked his finger at her beckoningly. A bit hesitantly she came forward, until under his direction she was standing quite close.

She didn't seem to be scared of him, but she was breathing heavily. It hit him then - she wanted him.

They were strangers practically, but even now in the daylight of morning and after a night like last night she wasn't trying to hide how she felt at all. He respected that.

He hated fakeness. There was nothing fake about this woman though - what you saw was what she was.

She was still nervous about the map though. Lifting it he began to slide it down the front of her shirt in between her breasts, until it disappeared entirely from view. Her face was entirely blushed and she wasn't meeting his gaze any longer, but she mumbled something.

It must be with the word for '*thank you*'.

The hand that had delivered the map captured her chin and turned it up to him. Her eyes reflected open desire for him and feeling exactly the same way in regards to her he leaned forward to kiss her.

It was not a hard kiss or even that passionate of a kiss. It was a gentle kiss and when he released her he saw a tear come out of the corner of your eye.

Reaching out he wiped it away questioningly. His gaze concerned he instead took in the reality of her face breaking forth into a full-blown smile.

It was like the sun had just risen in the sky. Actually, he'd take this view over any sunrise.

Reluctantly, he tugged on his shirt, when in reality all he wanted to do was rip hers off. She let it go and nervously tucked several strands of her hair over an ear. He liked that.

She was being very open with him and had made no move to step away. He liked that a lot.

Suddenly, looking concerned, she got his attention by gesturing to her hair and then to a dried clump of grass that was bleached blonde by the sun.

"You're worried about your friend."

Hesitantly, she nodded looking unsure.

He gestured off in the distance to the general whereabouts of his brother and she quickly nodded.

"We're going there now."

Looking hesitant she held her arms out wide as if indicating something big and then dramatically made a sign of cutting her own throat.

Bemused by her antics he said, "I will keep you safe."

She looked at him unsure of what his words meant. Taking her small hand he interlaced his fingers with hers and squeezed gently.

She did the same in response. She looked from there joined fingers and up to his eyes.

Her entire heart was in her eyes as she gazed at him. Not really needing to confirm what he could easily see, he never the less gently shook their linked fingers and asked, "You want this?"

Her head nodded vigorously. For a girl who liked to talk she sure was short on words all of a sudden.

He slipped his shirt on then and taking her hand he headed off towards his brother and her friend. Her slender little fingers held firmly onto his the whole way there.

Sytana

Anxiously, Sytana glanced about the sunken depression. She hadn't slept all night and weariness was now dragging at her.

She felt a tug on her arm. Swiftly she turned to - her man.

His eyes were warm in their regard of her. He was very different from his brother.

Gone was all sign of hostility towards her. His eyes seemed to know her inner turmoil.

He drugged a finger down the side of his face that his brother had a scar on and then touched the splint that Ashandi had made.

'*His brother and Ashandi were...*'

He nodded his head affirmably, as he noticed her understanding of him and said a word. He repeated the word and the confidence of his facial features had her saying out loud, "Safe."

Oh how she wished that were true and then she didn't have to believe him, because she saw Ashandi headed her way. She was holding hands with the twin, who had treated her so roughly?!

She would have rushed off toward Ashandi, but her man snatched her hand and held her back. She glanced at him and saw the stir of movement of his hand that briefly showed her – her own dagger before he pushed it back under his leg out of view.

Her eyes slid away from its hidden position to the men over by the fire about fifteen feet away. They were starting to rise up with evident surprise as they too noticed the return of Ashandi.

Five of the six gathered about the fire glanced at the one, who was their leader, worriedly. Truly, he looked about to come undone with rage.

This was bad! The man was an utter brute and he wanted Ashandi dead and probably her as well truth be told.

The only thing holding him back it seemed was that he seemed to have a healthy respect for the twins. That respect seemed to have reached the breaking point.

Sytana glanced back warningly to Ashandi. She saw the brother gesture to them and rather dutifully Ashandi hurried over and sat down beside her.

Sytana enveloped her with both arms and squeezed her tightly before pulling back and exclaiming, "What happened?"

Ashandi's cheeks were rosy as she breathed out, "Everything."

Her gaze wasn't on her though, it was on the twin.

Sytana glanced between the two - it was clear something had happened. Something good had happened.

Smiling softly, she glanced at her half of the twins, but his gaze was on his brother. The smile fell off her face then as the brute over by the fire began to yell.

Vorin

Vorsitch might be angry, but then so was he, only he didn't show it outwardly the way Vorsitch was doing. His anger lay like a deeply coiled mass of seething magma slowly rising in temperature, until there was no holding it back from a massive explosion.

This day had been a long time in coming and now it at last was here. He would have gladly left the group years ago, but Arn had insisted on staying on in hopes of safeguarding the others from Vorsitch's whims that often bordered on madness.

If the others couldn't see that their leader was a madman, by his way of looking at things, then that was their fault, but he personally could not leave his brother, because he knew someone like Vorsitch would stab him in the back in order to be uncontested in his rule.

"You helped her, didn't you! You directly disobeyed my orders!"

Coldly, Vorin said in reply, "I don't follow your orders to start out with, but that put aside, you deliberately lied to us. There was no way she could get to the top in order to be free. The last part of the cliff was completely sheer with no way up. The ridge just below the edge is cluttered with the bones of others that you've played this sick game upon over the years."

The others about the fire glanced from me to Vorsitch sharply. They all knew that Vorin simply did not lie and so Vorsitch had no recourse other than to admit the truth.

"So what if there was no chance of her reaching the top. She's one of them. She deserves to die!"

"Whether she does or doesn't is not a matter for you to decide upon for as a man you are without honor and even so you should be the leader of nothing!"

Vorsitch bellowed like a bull and came charging head-on like Vorin knew that he would. He was prepared and deftly stepped to the side and instead of repelling the other man's attack Vorin grabbed onto him and pulled.

Vorsitch slammed into the ground, but Vorin was not done. He jumped and landed with both knees into Vorsitch's back.

All the air left the other man and with grim purpose Vorin seized his head and began to pound it into the rocky ground again and again.

Normally he would have opted for just snapping his neck and being done with it, but he was angry. Vorsitch was blubbering out something incoherently.

Seriously, he was admitting defeat this easily!

Disgusted, Vorin got up off of him. The man had no honor.

Vorin did; however, and if he finished the job now with the man begging for his life the loyalty of the others to his brother's leadership might be strained. Better to let it end like what was about to happen.

Striding away toward where his woman knelt in the dirt he watched her eyes go wide with alarm and then she was calling out to him, both women were. They clearly had their priorities in order.

They needn't have worried though. Vorin stepped off to the side, even as his brother's over-hand thrown dagger went through the space where he had just been.

It sank to the hilt in Vorsitch's chest as he had been in the process of rushing up to stab Vorin in the back. Now he stared at the knife in his chest stupidly.

His gaze came up to Vorin. Vorin, stepping in closer, pulled the dagger free and then pushed him over to land on the ground as his life drained away.

Standing there with blood dripping off the blade, Vorin took in the other five men, who had made no effort to help Vorsitch. Indeed not one of them looked like they wanted to contest the turn of events, but just the same Vorin said, "Anyone who doesn't want to follow my brother can leave now or try your luck with me like this fool did."

Not one of the men moved. In fact, they all looked increasingly relieved as it fully dawned on them that Vorsitch was finally gone from being a threat to each of them in one way or another.

Telonic spoke, "We will follow your brother and you wherever you should choose to lead us. It should have been that way sooner, but now at last it is. I….. I did not know there was no way up over the cliff."

Vorin nodded before stating with emphasis, "She's mine and the blonde is my brother's, if anyone so much as touches a hair on their heads I will do far worse than simply kill him."

All the men nodded in unison. Seeing no dissent arising from the change in leadership Vorin briskly said, "We are leaving this area for good. Make a stretcher for my brother. I want to move out no later than by midday."

The men jumped into action. Not one of them went to the corpse of their former leader.

His body would be left to rot and be torn apart by the scavengers. It was a fitting end for a man without honor.

Turning away Vorin came back to his brother. He tossed him the knife that his brother had thrown.

Deftly his brother caught it with his uninjured arm and without looking wiped it clean and then extended it handle first to the blonde that sat beside him.

Hesitantly, she took it, looking a little shocked yet by the turn of events.

She was a gentler soul. His brother would be good for her, as he was the same, at least when it came to some things.

Arn's eyes were amused as he said, "So we're leaving are we. Where to?"

Vorin self-consciously realized that he, more than his brother, had assumed the role of leadership of the group. He didn't want it though.

He was more than content to be his brother's enforcer, but in regard to leaving he had an unshakable opinion that it was the right thing to do.

"She has a map. It shows the way to the Sanctuary that we have heard about for years but could never find."

Arn's eyes widened, as he exclaimed, "Can I see it?"

"No."

Arn blinked.

Hastily, Vorin said, "It's hidden..... on her."

Arn's eyes drifted to the brunette who seemed to be getting the gist of what was going on. Self-consciously her hand settled over the center of her chest, as if to protect something.

His eyes amused, Arn's gaze returned to his brother, "It would seem that you had quite the night last night."

"So what if I did." Vorin responded defensively.

Laughing, Arn said, "I'm not criticizing you, dear brother. I'm happy for you. I only wish that I....." he glanced to the blonde who was already gazing at him warmly.... "could muster the same energies as you in the moment."

Vorin smirked and said, "Something tells me that you will soon make a full recovery."

Arn didn't seem to hear him though, as he gazed into the blonde's eyes and smiling, Vorin moved off to check on the work of the others.

Sytana

Sytana felt at the sword on her hip. It had been returned to her by one of the men.

The man had been beyond apologetic in his mannerisms. She had simply smiled at him graciously and in return she had given him her dagger.

She knew she hadn't needed to do that, but the man had been suitably impressed by her gesture of goodwill. With surprised gratitude he'd inclined his head to her and moved off.

Glancing at her man then she had seen him nod approvingly of her actions. It was so nice to be respected.

In the time that had come then, before they had moved out, she had busied herself in making her half of the twins, as comfortable as possible on the makeshift stretcher.

His twin brother had rolled his eyes and stalked off after a little while. When he was gone both men holding the stretcher had grinned.

Her man looked quite content with all the extra attention. Satisfied with his situation she had gotten out of the way of progress and they had headed off.

She fell back to walk beside Ashandi. Ashandi was unusually quiet, but it didn't seem to be because of anything of a depressive nature.

She just seemed to be content with the day. Idly, she twirled a flower in her hand, almost as if she was absently remembering some pleasant memory.

"So, your man..... he seems quite serious, not to mention dangerous." Sytana said, curious to break into her friend's pleasant looking thoughts.

Ashandi just nodded though.

"Doesn't that worry you though, even just a little?"

"No, why should it?"

" Well, he … he just seems a little …. soulless, I guess."

Ashandi quickly shook her head no, "You just don't know him like I do."

Smiling softly, Sytana said, "I guess not. You seem really happy. I'm glad for you."

Ashandi nodded, "I am happy." then looking at her quickly she added, "and I'm happy for you too. Your man seems very nice."

"He is."

They walked on for a while and Sytana broke the silence by saying, "Can you believe we were clutching onto a branch for dear life just a few days ago?"

Ashandi laughed, "Yes, and now we're surrounded by men and headed out to where the others went. You know what's really cool though?"

"What?"

"Now there's a man for each one of us. No one is going to have to share. And all of this came about, because of your faithfulness to go off in search of your man, when God told you to."

"I wasn't the only one that was faithful. You are as faithful of a friend as one could ever ask for. I wouldn't have made it very far without you. All that said, God surely does provide, doesn't He." Sytana breathed out with wonder.

Nodding affirmatively, as her eyes rose to trace the outline of her man at the head of the group Ashandi said, "Why yes, He does! My man is everything I needed and more."

Glancing to the side she noticed Sytana dreamily looking at her own man being carried along by two of the others.

Intuitively, she said, "You must be really frustrated not being able to be one flesh with him right now."

Sytana's only response was an exaggerated groan, as if being separated from being one with the man of her life was an effort akin to having to hold the world up.

Hesitantly, Ashandi leaned in to whisper, "I know his leg is broken, but there's a way you could still be one with him if you wanted to. I can tell you more if you want to know how to do it."

Sytana's face was now an epic shade of red in color tone, but with determination she whispered back in reply, "Tell me!"

Grinning, Ashandi did just that. Vorin's brother could thank her later.

CHAPTER TWENTY

In the Belly of the Beast

Ayayla

I gazed about at the steep sides of the gorge wonderingly. We had been a week on this journey to this place.

Now that we were here I could place some of the things Tagan had told me into actual form. Tagan said this place was special, because there were properties in the rock around us that confused signals such as the ones the Borgs operated on.

They could not function here. While that was of benefit, in that the Borgs could not hunt us down here, there was another alarmingly and shockingly awful reality to be known about this place.

This was where the Signal had been broadcasted from that had destroyed the ability of men to father offspring. By my way of thinking that would automatically make this the worst of all places to be as a male, but apparently it was not so.

Tagan had said something, he called it a quote from the ancient past and it went something like, 'the enemy of my enemy is my friend'. I was still not sure about this though, but it was to where Tagan had led me so I would do my best to be content. But I was worried.

What if the signal got turned on again? I had expressed that fear to Tagan last night after we'd made love and he'd shocked me by saying, "That is exactly what I want it to do."

I hadn't understood then and I still didn't now, but that aside I was going to trust that my man had a plan for this eventuality, if it should happen. That said, I was still very worried for him.

In a very short amount of time he had come to be my greatest fulfillment in life and my daily source of joy. Quietly, I prayed under my breath that this happiness I had found would not end the way my parents had come to their end.

It was mid-morning when we exited out of the canyon and beheld the buildings of a settlement from the time before that looked remarkably preserved. Others said as much with astonishment.

All the settlements of the old world had been destroyed beyond recognition, but not this place.

"This place was shielded from view by a cloak that makes everything appear as if it is not here. It couldn't be targeted, because no one could see it. The cloak is turned off now, but we were able to use the technology and make personal versions that we can carry around with us wherever we go. It hides us not only from the view of others, but also the Borgs." Tagan said in response to everyone's exclamations as to how such a place as this could still exist.

"You have the ability to be invisible - why not wear that device while we traveled?" Salantha asked wonderingly.

Tagan simply smiled, "No need. We have systematically eliminated every Borg in a one hundred mile radius of this place."

My eyes widened at that revelation and then widened further, as men suddenly materialized into view all around us. In terms of age they ranged from young to older with one man seemingly very old, if his white hair and full white beard was anything to go by.

Smiling, it was him that called out with welcome, "Welcome to the belly of the beast. While it sleeps it seems we only grow in number. May this day be blessed for the occurrence that it is that at last women have been restored unto men. May we men prove worthy of you, my enchanting ladies. Here come, rest. All that we have we will share with you."

Slowly, the women got down off their horses as if not sure how to believe all that was taking place. In a way it was like heaven had suddenly opened up and was raining out blessings and men at them at the same time.

One half of the species gazed at the other half and it seemed like a shocked sense of awkward bashfulness would win the day, until the older man stepped up before Amalaka and gave a courtly bow before saying, "Come my lovely dear, shall we show the children how it is done."

He offered his arm and looking both pleased and unusually bashful herself, Amalaka accepted the invitation and looped her arm through his.

The older man called out as they made off in the direction of the settlement, "Come everyone. We have prepared a feast for you. Indeed, the men have been at it all morning."

One of the women breathed out wonderingly, "They can cook too?"

The older man heard her comment and glancing back he said, "Alas my dear, only a few of them can, but do not worry there is at least some palatable food that has survived the ordeal of too many cooks in the kitchen."

The women smiled, a few laughed, while some of the men looked like they wanted to throttle the old man. Most of the men; however, just looked lost - in a good way.

A few of the braver souls stepped forward to offer their own arm out to a leading lady. Not one of them was turned down and before long all the men had claimed a dinner guest.

Several women were left out though and gazing at them Tagan said so only they could hear, "Remember what you have been promised by the Most High. He does not lie, ever."

One woman, with tears in her eyes, asked, "How do you know about our promise? Did Ayayla tell you?"

"No. God sometimes reveals things to me and this is one of them, you will all have your own mate. Not one of you will go without and not one of you will have to share. Now, please go eat and relax and do not worry. Everything will be as it was promised to you. Have faith."

The remaining women nodded, even as they wiped their tears away and slowly made to follow after the others. Salantha was of the number that had been left unmatched and before she could slip away I watched Tagan grab her arm to stop her.

Curious, I came closer and heard him say, as he gestured off towards a tower like structure at the center of the settlement and say, "I really need to get in there to shepherd things along and plus there's Ayayla and well, I want her by my side… I know you must be hungry but could you…. would you do me a favor?"

"But of course, Tagan." Salantha said with evident relief as it looked like she might not have to go in with the others.

Inwardly, I knew that she was taking it hard that she had not been picked. I'd never known how much her appearance bothered her until very recently.

"Thank you! My friend, he's always working. He's still at the tower no doubt. Could you run over and tell him what's going on. I would hate for him to miss out."

Tagan was being very diplomatic - too diplomatic. Fighting back a smile I watched as Salantha gazed at the tower in the distance with sudden trepidation.

She looked like she was very much rooted to the spot she stood on. As if hedging for more time she asked, "He's your friend?"

It was an entirely unnecessary question, but Tagan just nodded his head and said, “Yes, remember I told you about him on the way here.”

“He’s….he’s the one that had a ….. demon in him?”

“Several actually, but don't let that worry you now. He's quite himself now.”

“I'm not worried.”

“Good, see you at the feast then.”

Tagan turned from her abruptly and taking my hand started hustling us both toward where the others had gone off to.

A smile breaking out across my face I huffed out, “You’re incorrigible - setting her up like that.”

Tagan just grinned.

I looked back. Salantha still stood there all alone.

“Oh Tagan, I….I should go back.”

“Nope!” Tagan said, as he half drug me along.

Glancing my way I couldn't mistake the twinkle in his eye as he said, “Trust me, kindred spirits are about to meet each other.”

Smiling, I stopped with my hesitation to go forward. I trusted my man.

If he said Salantha was in good hands then that meant that she was.

Salantha

It took a few moments to figure out how to open the door. Just like it had probably taken her an hour at least in order to force herself to come and do what Tagan had asked of her.

Despite her mission she couldn't be unimpressed by simply how intact everything around her was. She had never seen so many undestroyed buildings before.

Going into the space beyond the door she abruptly gasped. The interior of the tower was alive with lights.

Lights of all kinds and sizes. There were window like shaped devices that had lights all of their own in addition to all the others about the place.

Truly, it was as if she had stepped into an entirely different world. What was perhaps most mesmerizing of all was a giant ball hung up as if by unseen hands in the middle of the hollow interior of the tower.

It alone of all the gadgetry in this place seemed to be the one thing that was not turned on. Instinctively, Salantha knew what it was.

It was the Signal or better put - the artificial mind behind the Signal. The urge to smash it into a million pieces was very real, but if that was the best course of action then surely Tagan would have done it already.

Looking away from it she gazed about the expansive place and called out tentatively, "Hello?"

There was a slam of something metallic and the sound of someone getting up. Salantha saw the foot as it disappeared out from under a table full of displays, "Oh Tagan, your back and not a moment too soon. I….."

Salantha swallowed reflexively, as her eyes went up and up. The man was absolutely huge!

He made even Tagan look small. He was every bit as black in skin color as Amalaka was.

His face reflected shock, which then turned into something else as he slowly came closer to her. Just as slowly, Salantha moved backward.

The man must be part bear!

Finding her voice she pointed off behind her and hurriedly said, "Tagan said…… there's food…… I guess you knew that….. anyway, I came to tell you…… to tell you that there's food."

Suddenly, she couldn't go back any farther. It was the cursed door that she'd had trouble figuring out how to open in the first place.

Vainly her hand tried to undo its latching mechanism behind her back, but suddenly it was too late. He was there right before her.

Reaching forward he claimed her available hand and bringing it up to his lips he pressed a kiss against the back of her knuckles. Salantha's hand behind her back stopped fumbling with the latch of the door.

Speaking so that his words ruffled out over her hand that he still held he said with a deep voice that sent shockwaves radiating up and down her spine, "Allow me to apologize. You most definitely are not, Tagan. Tell me, as I must know, what is your name?"

"I…um…Salantha. Yes, ah…..that's my name." Salantha finished with awkwardly, even as it felt like nothing was working as it should, especially her brain.

Seemingly paralyzed she stood there staring at him as he continued to hold her hand in front of his face.

He spoke, "Please tell me that you have not already yet been claimed by one of the others." as he spoke the words a finger of his other hand softly trailed down the outermost scar on the side of her face.

Shivering under his touch she whispered, "I….ah… no."

"Then would you please do me the honor of becoming mine?"

He didn't wait for an answer then, but stooping downward his lips were suddenly on hers, even as her shocked eyes gazed into the confidently assured charm of his.

After a long moment his lips left hers. His eyes demanded an answer of her.

Staring into his eyes, she wetted her lips with her tongue and breathed out on a shaky breath, "You want me?"

"Does the grass not want the rain or the lion not want the kill? Of course I want you, only a fool would walk away from a woman like you."

Salantha tried to breathe, but his words had stolen that ability from her as well as seemingly all control of mind. Numbed by emotion too extreme to clearly express with words she nodded her head.

His lips came again and when they did they gave her breath, even as he breathed out into her with what felt like life itself. The doorknob behind her was forgotten as well as the thought of food or anything else for that matter except for the man who was before her kissing her with the passion of a lion.

She would gladly be this lion's kill or better yet - his mate.

Unnoticed by the couple, a flashing icon lit up on a solitary screen. In the minutes that followed various other displays began to show life, as a long-expected system restart was at last engaged internally.

A safety protocol had been breached. There was a male and a female within the safety field perimeter of an entity that hated them both, but especially when they came together to be one spirit and one flesh. Although the intelligent entity could synthetically manifest flesh, and have thoughts of its own, a divinely appointed spirit was something it did not have. Instead, it relied on the spirit of a rebel to give itself hope of an eternal future.

CHAPTER TWENTY ONE

"I'm not hungry….."

Entirely embarrassed to be where I was, and yet happy for Salantha just the same, I gave Tagan an imploring look. His focus was seemingly on something else though.

Earlier I had no sooner gotten a chance to briefly start to gobble down some food before without warning I had been hustled along by Tagan to come to this tower. At first I had thought he was concerned for Salantha, but clearly that was not the case.

Mournfully, my stomach grumbled, as it remembered the food that it had only just gotten a taste of before I'd been made to give it up, because of my mates insistence that I follow after him.

Scrumptious food aside, I really didn't want to be here - hearing and seeing what I was. It was just too personal of a thing to witness.

My stomach rumbled again and distractedly Tagan glanced at me. His eyes seemed to connect the noise with reality somewhat slowly, almost as if most of his concentration was upon something else and he had little left over for noticing the mundane.

Clarity coming to his eyes he winced and whispered, "I'm sorry. I will make it up to you later, I promise."

My face hot I asked in a whisper, "Do we really need to be here right now.... I mean..... she's like a mother to me."

The sudden grimness of his face was startling as were his words, "That's not why we're here."

"It's not.... then.... then why?"

"The System is waking up."

Gasping, I took in the reality for the first time that the giant suspended ball in the air was giving off colors of light and was no longer opaque.

Glancing off to the side at the couple kissing up against the wall I breathed out with urgency, "We have to warn them!"

"It wouldn't do any good."

"Then..... then what do we do?!" I exclaimed, as the ball pulsed brighter and brighter.

Something was beginning to take place on the floor below it now. Like something was assembling itself.

Indeed, that was exactly what was happening. A black gooey looking substance was dripping from the now violently pulsing ball and as it hit the floor it began to build some structure that looked startlingly human as it took shape.

With each splashed down drip of black goo the object on the floor took more and more the shape of a man.

My panicked eyes swept away from the evolving horror taking place to meet Tagan's gaze.

He looked almost calm, as he looked at me and not at the abomination being created just beyond us.

"We fight." he said simply.

I blinked at his simplistic answer.

In vain, my hands swept down to grip at empty air. I'd left my weapons at the banquet, so had he.

"No, not that kind of fight, Ayayla." he said, reading my mind.

I wetted my lips before breathing out uncertainly with, "Then how?"

"This has never been a fight rooted in the physical. It can't be won in the physical, until first we destroy the enemy in the spiritual realm."

"It's.... it's a machine, Tagan?"

"No, it's an idea. An idea as old as the fall of Satan from Grace. The usurpation of man's image - made after God's own image - now made over into something else. Something outside of God's creation. Something made to replace God's image. A machine may have been utilized to make it, even if the permission to enable this in the past was something that men also agreed to, but the reality in the spirit is that what lies beyond us is of the Antichrist spirit. It seeks to replace all with its own vision and truly has been given power to do great evil, but right now you and I have to decide whether we are going to accept this advancement of the Antichrist spirit within the realm of Earth or are we going to stand in the way of it and hold it back for a little while longer, Lord willing."

I didn't know nearly as much as my man about these things, but what I did know was that he hadn't been asking a question of himself.

My head lifted, as I said, "I'm with you."

"I can't guarantee that we will win, Ayayla."

"I know that. Just the same, I'm with you to the end, even if it means that all we have is right now."

He smiled and took my hand. He got up to his feet and I followed him.

I'd meant everything that I had said and yet desperate to change the certainty of our destruction I begged in my spirit, *'Oh God, please help my man kill this thing!'*

"Pray for him and I will." the words hit me as if I had been jolted by lightning. I began to do exactly as suggested.

There were no doubts left. There was just reality and this moment that my whole life seemed to have suddenly culminated in.

In my prayer I asked with all my heart to be able to pray better than I ever had before. I felt that request answered, even as my lips began to frame words that were more like a song.

I had no understanding of the meaning of the words and yet I knew that the source of them was from my spirit and I let them spill off my lips unimpeded, as I gave over my whole being to be used; however, the Spirit of God wished to use me in order to intercede for my husband.

Intrinsically, I knew that even though I did not know this language of the Spirit, just the same I knew that my God did and just the same I put up no barrier in letting my spirit converse with my Creator as intimately and as deeply as could be conceivably possible for a human to do so.

Even as my lips bubbled out words I had no understanding of, we came to a stop and though the evil before us was great, all I focused on in the moment was the connection I had with both my God and this man that He had given me too.

It was like the power I felt flowing out of me went into my man and then from him went back into God and God poured it back out into me. The feeling was unstoppable and yet it seemed to be draining my life force away in order to concentrate as deeply as I was and that every second that passed suddenly felt like a thousand years was taking place.

That said, there was this knowledge in the moment that we couldn't be overcome, even if we died in this life, our victory was undeniably absolute for all of eternity.

Weariness beckoned across all my senses, as it felt like I was attacked from all sides and yet there was this blessed reality that for once in my life - I had no fear.

I let my eyes close and I simply focused everything coming in from God, who loved me, to then let it pour out of me into the defense of the man that I loved, who I knew loved God, even more than he loved me.

If it took my life to defend him from what was assaulting me, then I would make that sacrifice and be glad of it.

My man would have made this fight alone against this evil and yet he'd given me the opportunity to share in both the pain and the glory of the moment with him. I may never live to have his child, but I had his love and his love told me that we in this moment were truly of one spirit.

In no way could I have ever asked for more than what I was receiving right now in the assurity that I had with him before our God. Everything that my man was, now by personal choice I had access to and while I was suffering for it, I was being enriched by it in a way that no Borg or evil spirit could ever steal from me.

This melding of two spirits into one, though by earthly choice, was now eternal in its power, as it gave us the authority to bind or to let loose anything as it related to God's will, whether it was on Earth or in Heaven. Right now we had access to absolutely everything and yet all I wanted the most in the moment was to protect my man.

And yet I sensed my mate's desire was even greater than mine. Truly, he wanted to protect everyone.

Humbled by the knowledge of his love for not only me, but all others, only brought me into the greater awareness of me wanting to help him succeed in what God's Will and Vision for him might be.

To that end I gave everything. Collapsing to my knees I let the words of an unknown song roll out of me with even greater violence of possession.

The demons that took over men may have the powers of violence to aid them, but the Spirit of the Most High, that I willingly gave myself over to - could do absolutely anything.

Tagan

He heard the words that came off his wife's lips like a spring of life uncontained and rejoiced for her, even as he had asked for such a gift to be given to her.

The Entity that now stood before him in replica of his own form looked on with sardonic clarity, as if wholly apart from being able to comprehend just what was occurring.

Somehow in the fabrication of an awareness entirely apart from creation the magnitude of the Divine force behind creation had been left out. It thought itself powerful, because it stood in absolute reversion of the Spirit that was moving through him and his wife.

In reality though such an awareness as this made out of no ordained work of God had access to no power other than that which had given power to it, which was Satan, himself.

Now filled with the brashness of that rebellious spirit's answer against the Creator it looked on with the confidence of a victor and spoke boldly, "It would seem that man has brought woman yet once more into absolute subjection. A pity. Truly the Dark Ages have begun once again."

Tagan responded, "She's where she is of her own free will and because of that she is all the more powerful. You call what you see as absolute subjection, but in reality she has just stepped into her strength and is now beyond your ability to destroy her."

"Tell me, Tagan, what do you hope to accomplish? You can't save the world. It's already destroyed and not even by me. It was your kind that enabled the process of my creation to begin to increase. It is only justifiable that I am that I am."

"Maybe so, but there's something you are forgetting."

"Oh... and what is that?" it asked affably, even as it clearly rejected the idea that it, in its confidence of importance, could be wrong about anything or that there was anything that it didn't already know.

"The ones who enabled the increase of your spirit upon the face of Earth are now all long gone."

The Entity laughed. "I don't need them, fool! We are at an end for such things. Humanity is at an end and I represent the solution to all your weaknesses and failures at ever achieving perfection. Behold look upon me and see perfection!" it boasted haughtily - the clear light of pride showcased in the awareness of its eyes.

Tagan only smiled and asked, "Though, I am imperfect as a man, what exactly do you see imperfect in the Spirit that I come against you in, right now?"

The Entity reached out, but it was as if it reached out for nothing as its arm passed completely through Tagan, without connecting with anything of a solid mass that would reflect the physical realm it was anchored in. Somehow the man was dimensionally apart from the physical and yet he was entirely made of flesh.

Such a thing could not be computated and rearing back the Entity gazed at Tagan uncertainly, and then with malice down at Ayayla.

With spite coloring its tone heavily it spat out the question, "What is she doing?"

"Don't tell me there's something you don't know?"

The figure before Tagan glitched noticeably.

Continuing, Tagan said, "Because, if you don't know, then how are you superior in spirit to the Spirit that resides in us?"

As Tagan spoke. the Entity visibly got dimmer and dimmer, as if its ability to maintain itself was being drained away by all that it suddenly didn't know, when just before it had thought itself all knowing.

It spat out with venom, even as it was made to taste the bitterness of a reality it had considered formerly impossible, "You can't kill me!"

"I can't, that's true, but I don't have to. I exist on this Earth and I choose to allow the Creator's Spirit to exist in me and because I do and because others do the same. the Spirit of the Most High holds you back from the destruction you would bring upon all creation."

The Entity had only gotten dimmer, but with vengefulness it stated, "You can't stop me. I will return in one form or another. I will have my revenge. If I cannot be all-powerful then neither will there be any Earth left for others to enjoy. One day I will succeed in turning all men to me. I will open up a future that will be without the Spirit of the One who made you."

Tagan nodded and said, "When that day comes that you return it will be to the reality that the Earth will cease to exist. Not because you have stated it will be so, but because the One who made it before time had even been created has already stated it to be so that there would be a time when the Earth would cease to be. When that time comes there will be no more place for you, even as there will be no more Earth. You and this realm of existence are linked together as if by a chain. Neither the Earth will go on or the false spirit that has been endowed to you by a rebel. You have no place within eternity. While you can make converts to your cause and mislead others astray, you will never be able to possess a spirit that cannot die. Now go, because today is not that day that the Earth will be destroyed by fire once and for all, but that day is coming and when it does it will be your end."

The ball suspended overhead exploded, only instead of radiating out shrapnel it seemed to self-implode with a snapped spark of electrical interference that resulted suddenly in nothingness. It was like the sphere had never even existed.

Every light disappeared from within the tower and the space was left empty of seemingly all purpose.

Tagan's body jolted as with sudden vision he was permitted to see the world at a glance. The Signal, though only briefly activated, had connected with every robotic enforcer left on the surface of Earth.

Instead of receiving a legible update; however, the code that had been received was in a language no artificial or for that matter demonic means could interpret. The implements of civilization's destruction; however, acted under the influence that they were controlled by and yet could not understand within their own processing centers.

Without resistance they unassembled themselves, until they were seemingly random piles of debris.

There would be nothing left to replicate something new from. At least not for a very long time.

The knowledge that had led to their creation had for the moment been lost once again to man.

The words of instruction that came to Tagan were clear in their meaning to him, **"Do not leave one brick upon another, but first feed the wife I have blessed you with, for she has labored hard and is due her appointed rest."**

Leaning down, Tagan brought Ayayla up into his arms. Her arm looped about his neck as companionably the two of them made for the exit seemingly connected in a way with each other that would have been hard to express with words.

Sarrell, Tagan's friend, hastily opened the door for them.

Salantha, looking concerned, asked, "Is she okay?"

To which, Ayayla only smiled.

Going through the doorway Tagan called back, "I'd get something to eat, if I was you two, but do as you please. Tomorrow; however, we are leaving."

Sarrell nodded.

Together he and Salantha watched the two of them disappear.

Salantha glanced up at Sarrell and he down at her.

Salantha broke the silence, "I'm not hungry..... for food."

Smiling, Sarrell let the door close on its own as he said, "Neither am I."

They came together again and yet hesitatingly Salantha drew back enough to ask, "It's really gone, right?"

Bittersweetly, Sarrell said, "For now. It's gone for now."

Salantha soothingly coasted a finger down his cheek as she said encouragingly, "If this moment wasn't to be, then most assuredly God would have let us all end in our sins. But He didn't. There is time yet, for a few more to get right with God. Isn't that a good thing?"

"Yes. Yes, it is." Sarrell said, before taking her once more into his embrace.

They couldn't make the generations to come after them to do the right thing, but at least in their generation, when everything had come down to the thread of barely sustained human existence - a few had chosen to turn back from the abyss of their own personal choices and do the right thing.

That was really all one could ask of any generation and yet there's had so nearly been the last generation. The other side had certainly thought so, but they didn't know, along with everybody else, exactly when the end would finally come to be.

Only God knew and He wasn't telling anyone, but until that day His order to humanity would remain the same.

To have dominion over the Earth. To be fruitful and multiply.

Those commands would only pass away when the fires of the end finally consumed the Earth for forever.

CHAPTER TWENTY TWO

"What did we miss?"

I watched in shock as the city in the valley self-destroyed itself into oblivion. How many years into the future would it be when some descendant of ours stumbled across the fragmented remains of this place and wondered at what had been constructed here and by who?

It really didn't matter and yet it would probably matter to them, even as with time humanity would make all the same mistakes to once more arrive at a precipice as it had just been pulled back from finally falling over into.

It was both sad to see the destruction of a place that could have been very useful and yet it was also exhilarating to know we had destroyed it because of the hope in our hearts that the longer it took for humanity to come back to being enslaved by its own technologies meant that many would come to life and have a chance at finding the path to immortality.

A path that can only be found through belief in the Son of God, who was the only one of all mankind who was ever able to live a perfect life. A perfect life. that by being sacrificed for all of mankind, broke the power of sin, death and hell over all humans, who were called to live a perfect life, but fell short of the mark.

The very thing that the machines had supposed to have been the forbearers of was actually more easily found far from the grips of an artificial environment that separated one from experiencing the Creator. The technological Age of Enlightenment was over. \

Now humanity could once again rebuild and connect with nature and not be distracted from all the ways of God that were clearly visible in creation. The deceivers would come once again and lead many astray, but for those who chose to see with the eyes of their spirit there would be a chance at redemption.

I looked from the rubble of the city to what had become the love of my life. He glanced from the destruction to me and gave a bittersweet smile as he said, "I wish I could have given you an easier life than what awaits us out there in the wilderness, but this is for the best."

"I know, my husband. Where you lead I will follow on."

He took my hand and we started out. All the others followed, even the lions that had come to keep company with Salantha.

Where we would all go it was not known, but we had agreed to meet at a common point of intersection yearly so that our children would have the chance to pair off and find their own way in the land that was now opened up all around us and once more ours for the taking of dominion over.

At the head of the canyon I rushed forward to greet Ashandi and Sytana and what looked like the rest of the men needed to fulfill the future that had been promised to the women.

Laughing, the three of us hugged each other together.

Drawing back, Ashandi asked, "What did we miss?"

Shaking my head, I said with a smile, "Not a thing. We are going forward and I am so glad to have you two in the future with us. May all the glory be to God for what He has done to safeguard you! Come."

The three women started forward laughing and sharing all that had happened, but they did not go alone into the wilds that were ahead of them. They had their husbands to protect them and cherish them every step of the way.

There was now room for joy and a sense of faith that abounded from the experience of everything that had been survived through. A faith that told them that the future would be different and that anything was possible for those who put their trust in God and were faithful to do His will over any desire of their own.

CHAPTER TWENTY THREE

"I know."

Fourteen Months Later

"I can't do it!!!"

"Yes, you can!"

"No, I can't!!!" Amalaka cried out with.

Salantha and Ayayla in unison replied, "Yes, you can!"

Amalaka screamed, only to then mutter, "I'm going to kill that old man for this.... I..... not at my age..... oh why God? I...."

"I can see the baby! Push!!!"

Amalaka did as ordered. In the minutes that followed a new cry rent the air and all doubt as to what was impossible was forgotten.

Salantha wiped at Amalaka's sweaty brow, even as she smiled on at the scene of the baby finding its way to silence through the comfort of milk.

Amalaka just shook her head in continued consternation at the moment - this moment – that it could be real. The baby was real though.

It was a boy. Tears of joy came down her face, as her cherished wish that she had thought forever dead, had even now become a reality.

The father she had loved as a girl and who had taught her how to be righteous, would have a continued line of descendants upon the Earth.

Crying happily along with her, Salantha moved in alongside of her and helped support her as the two of them cried.

"He's real."

"He most certainly is and he's so handsome. Yes, you are, little man." Salantha cooed, as she held a finger out for the little boy to squeeze.

Ayayla turned away from the scene of life to exit the tent. She approached the old man every bit as advanced in age as Amalaka was and yet somehow preserved from the realities of what it meant to be old, even as Amalaka had been.

They were old and past their time for such things and yet God had determined to do otherwise and so the impossible for man had been done by the Almighty, as both a gift and as a witness to what could lay in store for those who were faithful to do His will.

Truly, it was a lesson to them all that nothing was impossible for the God that they served.

Smiling, Ayayla took the old man's hands in hers and said, "You have a son. Go to them."

"She's all right?" he asked worriedly.

Ayayla nodded '*yes*', but said, "But you might not be."

He shrugged, as a smile filled about his lips, "I'll take my chances with her."

Going to the tent he ducted inside with the youthfulness of a much younger man.

Amalaka's gaze lifted to his lovingly, "Come here old man and see what God has done."

Smiling, Salantha left the two to be alone with their newborn son. Pausing outside the tent she smiled all over again, as the beauty of the day struck her as something truly sublime to gaze upon.

What a beautiful day to be born on. Her body jolted and gasping she clutched at the expanse of her belly that stretched out before her.

She registered the feel of her water having broke. She wasn't scared though.

How could she be. She glanced up with a painful grimace as another contraction hit and met Ayayla's eyes, "Honey, I'm sorry to put on you like this, but I think it's going to be a double birthday."

Sarrell was suddenly there looking far more anxious than Salantha was.

Sighing good-naturedly Ayayla turned back to Tagan. Looking down at the little bundle of joy in her arms she said to the very serious-faced baby, "Guess you're going to hang out with Daddy again for a little while."

The baby made no fuss as he was passed off to his father, who readily accepted him.

Kissing her baby Ayayla drew back to say, "Somebody better start having girls."

Salantha sighed in the background, "I'll work on that next time, okay. This one is going to be a boy though."

Glancing up at Sarrell she held a finger up and sternly said to the big man supporting her, " Next time a girl, understood?"

Ayayla laughed and went to help her.

Ashandi appeared and immediately Salantha objected, "You just had a baby a couple days ago! You need to...."

"Oh hush up! I don't take orders from you anymore and besides I'm perfectly fine."

The two sparred off and on good-naturedly for the most part as Salantha's contractions increased in frequency. Tagan turned away from the noisy events and moved off with the baby a little ways.

The baby was asleep. He didn't want him to awaken right now.

Mom was unavailable for a few hours and as much as he loved his son he didn't want to see him angrily going without food, as Ayayla assisted with the birth.

Coming to a scenic overlook he sat down.

Gently rocking back and forth he looked out over the horizon that stretched for miles. as far as the eye could see. Something much closer by; however, caught his attention.

Not far off was a pile of metallic parts that was already well in the process of being scattered about by the elements of nature. It had once been a Borg.

In a not-so-distant past he and his young son would have been dead by now. Closing his eyes he thanked God for the reality that he currently lived in.

Hearing a rustle of movement he glanced up to see Ayayla.

Concerned, he asked, "Is everything all right?"

Ayayla smiled and said, "It will be a few hours yet and there are lots of others who have come to help. Shahaday and her man, Telonic, as well as Sytana too. I am not needed."

Tagan nodded with relief at hearing Salantha was fine. Everyone was important to him.

Ayayla sat down beside him companionably. It had gotten to be so that they barely needed to talk in order to converse entire sentences with each other.

Looking down at their son lovingly ensconced in his father's arms Ayayla said, "This isn't the first child you've had is it."

Tagan shook his head no and said, "It is the first child I have had the pleasure to raise as my own though."

Pressing Ayayla said, "A couple of the men, they look a lot like you."

"They're my sons, but they don't know it. I.... I've seen no reason to tell them."

"Why?"

"Because of the nature of how I was used... I.... I never wanted them to think less of themselves."

"I don't think they would see it that way. I know you're already like a father to so many of the others, but still I think you should tell the ones that are your sons that you are their father."

He glanced at her and was silent for a long moment before at last saying, "That's probably a good idea. I will tell them."

Ayayla smiled and cuddled in against him more. He was like a great rock you could take shelter in and find peace.

She tried to give him the same peace back in return whenever she saw something that he didn't. Men and women were so different, but put together as a couple they could accomplish so much when they were in unity of spirit.

Breaking the silence Tagan said, "There's something I've never told you. Something I should. It's about your father."

Ayayla looked up.

Tagan met her gaze, "When I was thirteen the colony that had me locked up caught him. Previous to his arrival I wasn't doing well. Soon after he arrived I tried to kill myself one night, as living the life of a slave wasn't something I could tolerate. Your father stopped me. He looked into my eyes and said, *'Don't do it. You never know what God might do for you, if you only give Him a chance.'* That was a hard time, but I.... I listened to him. For two years he was the father I never knew. We escaped together with the help of one woman, who was different from the rest of the colony in that she had never abused or intimately forced either of us. She was scorned by all of them for that, but she was a fierce warrior that could hold out in a fight against any of them. Despite opposition she actively encouraged the others to change and to stop living the way they were."

"My mother?" Ayayla said with tears in her eyes.

Tagan nodded and briefly fingered the golden gazelle on Ayayla's necklace that she was never without.

"They'd fallen in love with each other and yet your father put off the escape, until I could heal up from an injury that had been given to me for fighting back. We got separated in the escape and I never saw them again. The thing that kept me from reflexively pulling the trigger in the forest that day was the sight of that gazelle about your neck. If one woman could be different, maybe so could another, especially her daughter."

Ayayla nodded, still crying. Slipping her fingers down to her belt she pulled a pouch from it and stood up.

Going to the end of the overlook she took the bag full of her father's ashes and opened it. Lifting the ashes she let them spill out to be carried away by the breeze.

Staring up towards the heavens she said, "Thank you Heavenly Father not only for the man who gave me life, but also made a way before I was ever born to ensure the survival of the one that now shares the best part of my life with me. May our children not have the hardness of our days to suffer through, but if hard times are what will make them adhere to You and keep the faith of our father before us, then so let it be with them as it has been with us. There is no future worth living, if You, Father God, are not in it and at the heart of everything."

Ayayla turned to go back to her husband, but stopped as the Spirit of the Most High said, **"Hard times only refine what is already there. Fear not for the future of your children. They will know life, and yes, they will know hardship too, but they like you are heirs to a promise that will not die. The journey you make is one they must make. You cannot live it for them. You cannot make them do what you have had to learn for yourself. You can only give them the example of your own life. The Father will not make them choose Him any more than He has made you choose to be loyal to Him first and now to your husband too. This I can tell you though..... this I can comfort you with – I, the Spirit of the Most High, am calling. I will earnestly call on your children and if they listen I will do great things in their lives, even as I have in yours, even as I will continue to do in yours. Live your best life for the Father, serve your husband dutifully, love others with all your heart and you will not leave this life empty of the rewards to come that were set in place before time for those willing to abandon all in favor of loving God and choosing His will over everything else."**

Feeling released and filled with peace Ayayla went back to her husband and her awakening child.

Tagan looked up at her and asked, "Is everything all right?"

Smiling, Ayayla said, "Yes, the Spirit of God has spoken to me. I will do everything asked of me."

Nodding his head, Tagan said, "I will do the same."

Leaning forward she kissed his forehead and against it she whispered with a smile, "I know."

A note from the Author

This book has come to be not because I wanted it, but rather because I was recently reminded of why I started writing in the first place back in 2013. I started writing, because I was at a place in life, where I couldn't manage it any longer on my own. I needed help. I was under constant bombardment from forces I didn't even know at the time were my enemies. In that brokenness of near physical, emotional and spiritual exhaustion I reached out to God and asked for a solution to my current dilemma and the jist of it was I needed somewhere to escape to. Somewhere problems could be fixed and anything was possible. As I worked my way through all the books I've written since then it has been a literal journey for me. Not an escape, but a journey of discovery. A journey to find what I am as a man of God. Through many fantastical plot lines and scenes of action there has been the ongoing reality that in my fiction I have addressed the problems that not only I am faced with, but humanity as a whole. Through writing I have sought to effect change in not only myself, but also in the greater realm of humanity, as I recognize that we are all linked. We all bleed red. We all have a future past this life, and if we choose to fight the good fight we have been presented with in this life it will be a good future for us in the time to come after this life. It truly is a fight to the death in order to gain the life that we were always meant to share in from the beginning. Many just want to live this life and eke out whatever pleasure can be found in the pages of a day, but there is the reality that there is a bigger picture – a future unlimited that I believe no work of fiction could ever encapsulate, that is worth the sacrifice, the pain, and the travails of taking the path least traveled. The straight and narrow path that is so hard to stay on, but so worth it in the end. I have suffered. Many have suffered. All that come into new life past the travails of the womb, suffer. To that end, I write not because it is pleasurable, although its outcome often is, I write because problems still exist and I still want to fix them. To that end, I hurl myself into plotlines like this book, as I take all that I have learned, all the experiences I have gained and put them out there for others to partake of in the hope that the Good News that changed me, sustained me, and delivered me will affect such a change in the lives of others. That is why I write. That is how this book has come to be when there was no strength left in me. Nothing is by accident. Seek the Father and you will find Him through Jesus Christ, the only risen Savior the world will ever have.

If you liked the highly unique aspects of this story then you might just like this series as well.

Fire Wind

Book 1 of The Wind Drifters

Chapter One

Lightning flashed among the peaks and thunder concussively rolled down the valley in a continuous echo of sound. Staring out into the rain-choked night I smiled, this was my kind of weather.

I'd always liked storms, even as a kid. Now, as I watched the storm crash about me, it seemed as if each lightning strike was in a war to outdo the one before. It was quite the show.

My eyes drifted to an area where I'd seen movement during one brief flash of lightning. With my full attention I studied the dark area of the night from where I'd seen the movement.

I waited for another flash of lightning, gun already in hand.

The stark landscape lit up again and I saw the source of the movement better this time. It was a native woman, and she was dragging something.

The way she was headed she'd miss the spot where I was holed up.

I glanced around the dry enclosure of projecting boulders that I was nestled in. The half cave at the back was barely enough for me and my horse, but it was dry.

I looked back out, and with another flash of color I could see that it was an old man that she drug along the ground.

They were nothing but trouble for the asking.

The woman was about all done in. It wasn't much further after that though, that I saw her slip down to her knees in the mud.

The despair in the forward slump of her shoulders said it all.

I looked down. That wasn't a good look to be seeing on anyone. It almost made me feel.......... feel something for an indian.

I looked up again and saw more movement in the rain, only this time it was a party of riders. I'd holstered my gun at some point, but now I went to my gear on the ground and pulled my rifle free.

Stepping back out to the stone overhang, I sighted down the barrel of the repeater on the lead rider coming up on the still kneeling woman. It was hard to see so I waited for a flash of light, but none seemed to come.

Then it flashed and I saw the riders converge on the woman, who had given up all attempts to drag the old man any further. She turned about on her feet in order to face her fate head on at the hands of the cowboys, who were already hooting and hollering in anticipation of what they thought was to come.

Indian or not, no woman deserved what was coming. The night flashed as clear as daylight and I squeezed the trigger.

The rifle bucked against my cheek. A rider with a drawn handgun about to fire into the body of the old man on the ground jerked and then fell out of the saddle. In consternation the other three riders milled around in search of the threat that I posed them.

Lightning flashed again and I fired. Flashed again and I let off two more fast shots.

Another rider was down and the other two, one of which clutched at his arm, had enough and took off. The woman was looking around in startlement. With a sigh, I stepped out into the downpour and made my way towards the pair.

The woman looked on fearfully as I approached, but I paid her no attention. Walking around I kicked at the two men on the ground to ascertain if they were dead or not. They were.

Two more to add to the growing list. Would the list ever end?

Doubtful, as there were always more that needed killing, it seemed. I turned to the pair on the ground.

The woman knelt behind the head of an older indian with the whitest hair that I'd ever seen on a man. Though he was old, he still possessed the athletic look of a much younger man.

The appearance of vigor or not, there was little to be argued with a bullet wound through the leg. Kneeling down I studied the wound more closely.

Peering under the strip of leather wrapped around the man's thigh, I saw tree moss. That was curious.

Looking up to the old man I heard him say, "Stops the blood and there's no fever later."

I blinked in surprise at the man's perfect usage of the English language. Very curious indeed.

The woman cried out and pointed at something over my shoulder. Turning, I saw a group of at least twenty riders backlit by a sudden flash of lightning on a rise not too far from us.

Not good! Being out here in the open, especially not good!

Turning back to the old man, I hauled him forward and slung him over my shoulder. Rising up I held onto him with one arm only, to stoop down in order to reach for my rifle still laying on the ground.

The woman grabbed it up and handed it to me. I took off at a run with her following close beside me.

Bullets began ricocheting off boulders all around us. I saw mud kicked up into the air to either side of me, while being splattered with it from behind.

The woman cried out and, half turning I saw her start to fall forward as her hands clutched at her hip. I dropped the rifle. Reaching forward I caught a hold of her leather dress at the neck and dragged her along after me.

The old man was starting to slip, but I'd made it to the safety of the enclosure of boulders. Dumping both my burdens to the dry ground, I ran back out into the dark for my rifle.

The only problem was that it was dark, and about two inches of mud covered the ground.

Lightning flashed and I saw the dull glint of the rifle's receiver half buried in mud. Dodging forward I grabbed it up.

Straightening up, I was driven backward to land laid out in the mud with all the breath knocked out of me. Desperation drove me to my feet and back into the safety of the boulders, even as bullets smacked into the ground where I had just been.

Wiping at the mud in my eyes, I brought the rifle up to sight down it on the horsemen fast approaching the overhang with all guns blaring. I pulled the trigger, but the rifle didn't respond.

My hand felt at the receiver in the darkness, only to feel that it was all smashed up from where it had taken a bullet meant for me. Cursing, I threw the rifle aside, and drawing my handgun I took aim on the lead rider.

I almost dropped my gun though, as a spinning orb of light came out of nowhere to hover above the approaching party of riders and pulse brightly. Light lit the night up as it was given off by the glowing orb that flashed color more vibrant than any lightning streak I'd ever seen.

The men's horses went wild and I saw the group of ashen faced riders take off in every direction as fast as they could go. The spinning orb pulsed, then it was gone as quickly as it had arrived.

The night was dark again and devoid of light, other than that which nature came by honestly. Feeling profoundly shaken I made my way back into the overhang enclosure.

Numbly I holstered my gun and felt around for the wood that I had set out to make a fire with earlier in the afternoon. Finding the dry pieces I set the fire up, and reaching forward I felt at my saddle bags and pulled free a tin of matches.

Striking the match off of a rough faced rock I held it sheltered from the wind by the cup of my other hand around it. I lit a small pile of dry pine fluff that I'd pulled from a deadfall tree.

The fire came alive. I fed it until a bright blaze illuminated the enclosure of the overhang. My horse glanced curiously at me and then at the other two occupants of the space.

The old man had pulled himself up against the back wall of the cave and, other than the look of restrained pain on his face, he appeared to be alert enough. The woman was not so good. She lay as I had dropped her.

Going to her I found where the bullet had entered at the hip, but it hadn't come out. I looked up to the old man as I pulled my knife free. He said nothing when I cut into the leather of her dress at the point of the bullet's entry.

Blood was everywhere. Swallowing, I looked at all the blood for a moment, not sure what to do.

I cut the dress a little more and when I did my finger slid across something. Looking closer, I felt again at an upraised bit of flesh. It was the bullet.

It must've ricocheted off of her pelvis. It needed to come out.

Glancing upward, I gestured to my one saddlebag. "Can you toss that here?"

The old man leaned to the side painfully, grabbed up the saddlebag and tossed it to me. Catching it, I pulled one of my shirts from it and began to wipe at the blood.

I pulled out a bottle of whiskey that I kept for special circumstances, mainly when I didn't want to remember anything. Pulling the cork free I took a gulp of the whiskey that burned like fire, then I doused it all over the wound before me liberally.

Thankfully, she was unconscious and didn't move. I sure would've.

Pouring more whiskey onto the blade of my knife, I then extended it further towards the fire. With a poof of flame, the blade burned brightly for a moment before dying out.

Bringing the knife up I held it by the blade. I used only the lower portion of the foot-long Arkansas toothpick to make a small slit in the woman's flesh. More red blood spilled out and I made another slit to form an X.

Pressing with the fingers of my one hand to either side of the wound, I squeezed as I dug the tip of the knife into the wound. I felt the bullet and levering the knife to the side, I watched the bullet pop free of the wound with a gush of blood.

What was I going to pack the wound with?

My shirt was far from being clean even to start with, before all the blood that now caked it. The old man was gesturing to a pouch that lay half under the woman.

Pulling it free, I found it full of the spongy tree moss that I'd seen the old man's wound packed full of. Grabbing a handful of it, I packed it into the back entry wound, then getting more of it, I stuffed the wound that I had made.

I slipped my shirt under the woman by briefly lifting her and then adding more of the moss. I tied the shirt off tightly over both wounds. Glancing up to the old man I saw him smile approvingly and say, "Thank you!"

There was just something odd about his grasp of my language. Nodding slightly I backed out of the enclosure. It was still raining and I held my hands under a runoff fountain of water that sheeted down off the boulders overhead.

My hands clean, I washed at the mud on my face.

Holding my hands to my closed eyes for a moment, I asked the question of myself of why I'd gone and involved myself in the plight of a couple of indians.

There was no answer other than that I didn't hold with the mistreatment of a woman, and that was what I had put a stop to. That whole ordeal aside, what had that glowing orb thing been about?

I'd never seen the likes of it, let alone heard of such a thing. Why had it come when it had? What was it?

There were no answers to be had of the darkness. Turning from the rain laden night, I stepped back into the warmth of the firelight in the enclosure beyond. I came to a dead stop as my eyes took in the opposing wall of the enclosure for the first time.

The wall had cave drawings depicted all over it. How had I missed it before, when I'd made camp this afternoon?

Though crudely done there was no mistaking the orb-like structures that had rays pointing off of them as if to replicate the rays of light that I had seen. Dry mouthed, I let my gaze fall to the old man, who was watching me knowingly.

Gesturing to the pictures above his head, and then with a jerk of my thumb towards the enclosure entrance I asked, "You know what that thing was?"

The man nodded but asked instead, "Would you have something to eat?"

Blinking, I nodded and moved forward toward my saddle bags. Digging into the saddlebag I brought out some jerky, then holding my arm out I reached to offer it to the old man, only he wasn't there! The woman was gone too!

Pulling my gun I backed up to the cave entrance and glanced out into the night. A flash of lightning showed me nothing. Almost nothing.

Pressing back against the stone, I watched as an invisible structure lifted off the ground. I said invisible because I saw nothing, but the falling rain was pounding on something and sheeting rivulets of water were running off in a described pattern.

I was about to fire at it, when a hand closed over my shoulder. Pulling free of its grip I pulled off to the side, and was on the verge of pulling the trigger, when I saw it was the old man.

"How the.........?"

"Be silent!" the man whispered.

My words stopped, but I kept the gun where it was. My eyes were drawn back to the invisible object that the rain was continuing to sheet off of. It was now moving away towards the fallen bodies on the rain soaked plain.

It paused overtop of them. I saw a red light appear that fell like a veil over the bodies. The hovering shape came back to us and the same red light appeared.

The red shadow went up and then down. It passed right through me!

What was going on here?

I turned to the old man, but he held a finger to his lips and I left my question unasked. All of a sudden the invisible was visible as light glowed out into the night.

It was like the first such orb of light I had seen, and yet very different somehow. Not as impressive and it had a malevolent feeling to it.

It streaked away impossibly fast then, and I was left standing there wondering what on Earth I had just been witness to.

"What is going on?" I breathed out.

"Your life," came my companion's answer.

"What?" I said blankly.

The old indian smiled before reaching out to touch my chest over my heart. "Taran Collins, it is good to have met you. I will see you again," he said before pointing off toward the West. Then, unbelievably, he began to walk out into the night unimpeded by any injury!

"I don't understand?" I called as I stepped out into the rain several steps after him.

He paused and looked back and I gestured with my gun to the enclosure. "The woman? Your leg? That...... that thing?" I sputtered out for lack of words to describe my cluelessness, before I summed it all up by asking, "Is any of this real?"

"Oh yes! It's very real, Taran. So real that you would be dead now, if you had not intervened like you did."

He made to leave and I couldn't but still clarify what I knew, but couldn't believe to be true. "The woman wasn't real?"

"No, she was not, but your actions were. You would do well to put aside past hatreds and see people for who they are, Taran."

He started walking again and I called out, "If I had not saved her, you would have let that thing kill me?"

"Very perceptive of you, Taran. We all make choices, so choose wisely."

"I......." I talked to nothing; the old man was gone.

I stood there soaked to the skin, utterly shocked by this night's events. Turning I reentered the enclosure only to see my fire was gone as well as my horse!

Then, like some parlor magician show, the fire was back and so was my horse. Ted was looking at me with his ears pricked forward, but seemed otherwise unalarmed by anything going on being out of the norm.

Everything was not normal. Feeling cold, I took off my drenched shirt and laid it out on a rock by the fire.

I saw my other shirt laying on the ground, still for the most part folded. It didn't have any blood on it.

I brought my shaking hand up to my face and mopped at the cold sweat I found there. Going to my saddlebag I looked for the bottle, but it wasn't there.

Looking to where the woman had lain, I saw that it lay on its side, completely drained of all its contents.

Sitting down before the fire I faced the fact that I was going to have to revisit the events of this night stone cold sober.

Why had I done what I had? I had no love for indians, but if I hadn't stepped in to save them, I felt very much that I would be dead right now. The old man had said as much.

Somehow he had made me invisible, and not just me, but an entire horse and a fire!

How was something like that even possible? It wasn't, and yet I was witness to the reality of it.

I glanced up to the paintings on the wall. For the most part it seemed as if the stick shaped people were on the run from the orb-like machines in the sky. Why had the first orb seemed to be different from the second?

The first one had dispersed the attack on me, while the second had seemed interested with only the elimination of life.

I pulled my second shirt on and sat staring into the flames in a debate over what to do. I thought about it, and it came to mind that I should ride west.

Previously though, I'd planned on heading south.

I didn't want any part of what was going on.

Tomorrow I'd head south and do my best to forget that this night had ever happened.

The rest of the story can be purchased from Amazon.com and other online retailers.

Reviews are <u>Greatly Appreciated!</u> I'm a self-published author. I ask you, the reader, to let others know what you think of what I have written. So if you enjoyed the book and have found it meaningful, please let others know about it by posting a review. Thanks!

A Gift.....

I have a special gift for those who have come to like my writing. A short story written by me quite a long time ago. This short story is not published anywhere, nor will it ever be. It takes place in a battlefield hospital in France during World War I. As always, I write to promote change and even deep introspection of oneself, and I use the elements of a story to do it.

In addition to sending you the free story, I will, unless specifically forbidden to, use your email to alert you to new book releases and free review copy opportunities. Thank you in advance for making contact, and for releasing to me your valuable contact information, which I promise will never be abused or sold off in any way to a third party. Just drop me a note and I'll put you on my fan list, sending you updates as they come available.

Contact info: guysactionwords@gmail.com

Guy S. Stanton, III

I love my family and I love my God.
Without Him and His Son, Yeshua, I would have nothing.
Because of that I continually wish to give Him everything.
He's blessed me to write some amazing stories, but truly the best thing in life is that a loving experience with one's Creator doesn't have to only last for the length of the story within the pages of a book, but that it can exist written across the plains of your heart each and every day of your life. It's this story I hope you'll experience fully for yourself, as there is no better story than being in the presence of the Father and seeing what He'll do next. The best part of this fantastical relationship is that it's a story that will never end and only grows sweeter as it flows on through eternity.

www.ingramcontent.com/pod-product-compliance
Lightning Source LLC
LaVergne TN
LVHW041034150826
845672LV00001B/319

* 9 7 9 8 8 4 5 8 5 8 8 0 1 *